REAPER

A MONTANA BOUNTY HUNTERS STORY

DELILAH DEVLIN

Copyright © 2017 by Delilah Devlin

All rights reserved.

No part of this book may be reproduced in any form or by any electronic or mechanical means, including information storage and retrieval systems, without written permission from the author, except for the use of brief quotations in a book review.

First, thanks Elle James for pushing me to write this book and inspiring me every day!
Next, I'd like to thank two people who helped me with some niggling details:
Mike F. and Kelly H. Google is not God; my friends know everything!

ABOUT THE BOOK

Former Marine, Reaper Stenberg is a bounty hunter, running his own satellite agency of Montana Bounty Hunters, along with his partner, Jamie Burke. As a general rule, Reaper doesn't like working with a partner, especially female partners. When chasing a bail-jumper, he prefers to keep his head down and follow the leads. He doesn't like the "chatter" that usually accompanies working or spending time with a woman.

However, partnering with Jamie has taught him a few things. There are women who can focus on the job at hand without letting silly distractions get in the way of his concentration. Jamie is one of those rare creatures who doesn't gossip, doesn't get into his business, and can actually be useful when shit goes sideways and they have to get physical. Over the months since their boss, Fetch Winter, put them together, Reaper has come to admire the woman's grit and ingenuity.

And then Jamie up and gets busy planning her wedding...

See what happens when Reaper has to deal with a ride-along author, Carly Wyatt, who—when shit goes sideways—proves his first female partner's grit and ingenuity aren't just lucky happenstance, and who challenges Reaper's strict relationship rules.

AUTHOR'S NOTE

The idea for writing stories about bounty hunters came to me when I was searching for an idea for a special project my sister, Elle James, asked me to be a part of. I agreed—and flailed for weeks trying to find just the right theme.

Then one day, while I was babysitting a very rambunctious toddler (not writing or even thinking about writing), I surfed through TV channels and landed on *Rocky Mountain Bounty Hunters*, a reality show on some cable network. I sat entranced for three hours, watching back-to-back episodes. Before the end of the first one, I was already making notes and getting really excited, because I knew this was something I could write.

I practiced, as I do, by first writing a bounty-hunter short story. *I'm giving you that story at the end of this book, so don't go scrambling to find it.* Writing that short story, I was hooked!

I didn't intend to write much humor into these stories, but after researching and over-indulging in many,

many cable network series, all featuring these rugged anti-heroes, I concluded that humor was inevitable. I hope you see why.

And if you love this new world I've created, let me know, because I'd love to write more stories about these men who live by a different set of rules—mostly inside the law but always according to their own unique sets of principles.

CHAPTER 1

As a general rule, Reaper Stenberg didn't like working with a partner, especially female partners. When chasing a target, he preferred to keep his head down and follow the leads. He didn't like the "chatter" that usually accompanied being paired with a woman.

However, partnering with Jamie Burke had taught him a few things. Women existed who could focus on the job at hand without letting silly distractions get in the way of *his* concentration. Jamie was one of those rare creatures who didn't gossip, didn't mess in his business, and could actually be useful when shit went sideways and they had to get physical. Her methods for subduing a target weren't ones he'd ever employ, but she knew how to compensate for her smaller frame and lesser strength. Over the months since their boss, Fetch Winter, had put them together, Reaper came to admire the woman's grit and ingenuity.

Case in point was their present predicament.

No, this time she hadn't tripped bail jumper, Mark Rebos, with a Jackie Chan move, and no, she hadn't gripped his balls and twisted so hard he begged for mercy. This time—while she'd run all out—she locked a cuff on her right wrist, jumped onto his back, and snagged his right with the other cuff. Now, they faced each other, squinting in the rain and ankle-deep in mud, and Rebos couldn't swing without dragging her closer.

The big man looked ready to explode. His pockmarked face was red, and his eyes bugged. Although Rebos was six inches taller than Jamie, and outweighed her by about eighty pounds, Reaper's money was in Jamie.

Rebos tried to draw back his arm, but Jamie flopped like a ragdoll, making him pull her weight around. He was tiring. "What the hell did you do that for?" he asked, his voice thick with frustration.

Still breathing hard, Jamie shrugged. "Your wrist was the only thing I could reach. And you're fast. I had to jump on your back before you pulled too far ahead. I was *not* running the length of Main Street again."

They were both drenched. Rain fell in sheets around them. When Reaper and Jamie had spotted Rebos leaving the tobacco store at the other end of Main, Reaper had no other option than to halt in the middle of the street while Jamie leapt out the passenger door. Thursday night in Bear Lodge, Montana was Bingo night, and the old folks had filled every parking spot along the street. He'd driven around the corner to park before following Jamie, who chased Rebos and yelled at the top of her lungs, "Fugitive Recovery Agent, dipshit!" Luckily, Reaper had time to draw a rain poncho over his head before speeding after them.

When she'd leapt onto Rebos's back, she'd taken him to the ground in the middle of a deep, muddy pit dug out by the torrent of water falling from the culvert above.

"You need any help, partner?" Reaper drawled, standing under an awning on the sidewalk above them.

Jamie bent and placed her hands on her knees, which forced Mark to double over. Their heads bumped.

She angled hers to frown at Rebos. "You gonna give me any more trouble?"

Rebos shook his head. "Just unlock these," he said, lifting their hands. He squinted at her in the deluge. "Hey, you're that female bounty hunter, ain't you?" he said, a slow grin stretching his mouth.

"I'm a *fugitive recovery agent*," she said, and then she strained to reach her left hand across her body to root inside her right front pocket.

When her shoulders dipped, Reaper grinned. "Lose your key?"

"I think they're in yesterday's pants," she said, her voice rough with disgust.

Reaper couldn't help chuckling, which earned him a mean scowl from Jamie. He held up his hands. "All right. I have a key." He reached into his left pocket, dug around, and then frowned. "Wrong pocket."

"Reaper..." she said, her lips tightening.

Yeah, he was just kidding. He reached into his right and pulled out a key. "Children, hold up your hands."

Rebos snorted.

Jamie gave him the evil eye.

Reaper was feeling pretty good about this capture. He hadn't had to bust a nut. And Jamie had provided him with a nice tale to share around the office. He unlocked the cuffs then pulled Rebos onto the sidewalk.

Jamie waved away his hand and climbed up on her hands and knees, before straightening her backbone and marching away.

Reaper wrapped his arm around Rebos's shoulder and gave him a little shove forward. They had a ways to walk. "So, buddy, did I read your arrest warrant right—you stole the sheriff's car?"

The big man shook his head. "How was I supposed to know that piece of shit Hyundai was his?"

Reaper patted his shoulder again. "Bad break, man. Hey, I'm gonna have to cuff you before I put you in the car."

"Yeah, I figured." He held still while Reaper moved behind him and snapped the cuffs around his wrists. "So, tell me. The chick, your partner...she single?"

Reaper was beginning to feel like it was Christmas. "She is." Not a lie. Jamie's wedding was in two months.

Rebos straightened his shoulders and thrust out his chest. "Think she'd wait for me?"

Although he wanted to, Reaper didn't dare laugh.

BACK AT THE OFFICE, they dropped their copy of the jail's paperwork on Brian's desk.

Brian was still bent over in his wheelchair laughing, his brown eyes tearing. Every time he glanced up at Jamie, he burst out laughing again—and he still hadn't heard about lovesick Rebos.

As he stared at the muddy mess she'd made of the floor, Reaper shook his head. From the top of her blonde head to the heels of her cowboy boots, his partner was coated in sludgy muck. "Think your boyfriend Sky's gonna let you in the house, looking like that?"

Her lips curved. "I imagine he'll make me strip on the front porch."

Reaper glared. Damn, sex on the porch sounded nasty. And fun. He didn't need a reminder of the fact his latest place to crash had reclaimed her spare key. Something he'd mentioned to Jamie that morning in the spirit of "sharing." Women seemed to like that shit, but Jamie hadn't commiserated. No, she'd raised her fist to Girl Power and told him he needed to find himself a *real* girlfriend. One he'd actually have to talk to. Reaper had shuddered at the thought.

He patted his pocket for keys, then began to turn, ready to head to the door. He had places to go—well, the nearest bar. Maybe there he'd find his next bed to crash in.

"Not so quick," Brian called out.

Reaper pivoted back and raised an eyebrow.

"Fetch has something special planned for you."

Reaper glanced at Jamie who was busy wiping mud off the side of her neck with a tissue.

"Not her. She's off for the next few days. Wedding stuff. You," Brian said, and then smiled.

Sometimes, he really couldn't stand Brian. Their office manager was part of Team Jamie. That smile was too wide and held more than an ounce of snark. "What's he want me to do?"

"You have a ride-along for the rest of the week, starting in the morning. An author friend of his."

For fuck's sake... Reaper groaned. "Why me?"

Brian's smile was angelic. "No clue. But he said you're to behave."

Reaper scrubbed a hand over his face. Fetch shouldn't have said that. Didn't he know better than to throw down that kind of challenge? "*Author*. Huh. He better not be late, or I'll leave his ass behind with you."

"Not a he..." Brian laughed again.

Reaper flashed a look of disgust at Jamie who chuckled softly. *No way in hell.* Training Jamie not to get herself killed had taken every bit of his patience. He didn't have any left for some author-*ess* who wanted to pick his brain and ask asinine questions, and who wouldn't know how to keep the hell out of trouble. No way. No how. Reaper fisted his hands on his hips and glared. He'd just have to make sure that a single day spent in his company was long enough.

With their laughter following him out the door, Reaper slogged toward his SUV through four inches of water accumulated in the parking lot. Once seated behind the wheel, he let out a deep breath and let his head fall back against the headrest. Not a bad day. Still, he felt... He didn't quite know. Restless, maybe? Dissatisfied? And why? Everything was going great. His success at Montana Bounty Hunters, as well as Jamie's, had led Fetch into trusting them to open and run this satellite office. Already, the operation was showing a profit. He liked his crew. Sure, he'd given Jamie a hard time when they'd started working together, but she'd more than proven herself over the months they'd partnered. Her friend Brian, even if he did get under Reaper's skin, was a good man and great support. He made their lives easier in measurable ways, handling much of the computer end of their job—a task Reaper didn't love.

Work was great. His crew was great. Soon, they'd add more agents. So, why wasn't he happy? Maybe Jamie was right. Perhaps, he needed a special someone in his life to give him something to look forward to when he walked out the door at the end of the day.

Or, maybe, he was simply pissed Sylvia had kicked him to the door the minute he made a face when she asked who he was taking to Jamie's wedding. Like she expected him to ask *her*. Fact was, he hated weddings, and the thought of taking a woman he "dated" to an event like that made him feel as though a noose tightened around his neck. So yeah, he'd grimaced.

"Crap. Why am I such a fuckup?"

His phone lit, and the strains to White Buffalo's "Come Join the Murder" filled the cab. What did it say about a man when the bartender at his favorite watering hole had his own ringtone? "Yeah, Brady?"

"Uh, Reap, you need to get on down here. I just cut off your brother."

Which meant Sammy was getting ugly. "Hell, I'm five minutes away." He tapped to end the call, hit the ignition button, and sped out of the parking lot. Sammy, drunk on his ass, usually ended up with a pricey bar bill for broken windows and splintered furniture—if not jail time in the county lockup.

When Reaper arrived at the bar, he removed his holster and secured it in his glove box. He also stored his badge.

Inside the bar, a fight was already in progress. Members of Sammy's motorcycle club stood in a circle around Sammy and another club member, Blacky McNally. Standing a head taller than most of the men crowded tightly around the staggering pugilists, Reaper made note that the fight must have just started because neither man was bleeding.

Brady waved to catch his attention.

Reaper circled the edge of the cheering crowd to reach him. "How'd it start this time?" he shouted.

"Sammy groped Blacky's old lady."

Reaper sighed. Sammy was looking to get his ass kicked. "I'd appreciate you holding off calling the cops."

His arms crossed over his burly chest, Brady nodded. "I know you'll make it right."

So much for his cut of tonight's takedown. Reaper sighed and pushed his way through the crowd.

"Hey, it's the bounty hunter," one of the club members shouted.

"It's Fugitive Recovery Agent, dipshit," he muttered, and then smiled. "Unless a bench warrant carries your name, you got nothing to worry about." He rolled his shoulders, raised his fists, and then waded in.

Reaper's heart rate sped. Not one to ponder the vagaries of fate, he couldn't help the little uptick of satisfaction that lightened his mood.

A fight on a Friday night was almost a Stenberg tradition.

A HOUR LATER, Reaper tossed a bag of frozen peas onto the kitchen table in front of his brother then pulled out another and took a seat opposite Sammy. Without speaking, because he really didn't want to start a shouting match, he squeezed the bag between his hands to loosen the frozen vegetables. Then he set the bag on the tabletop and rotated his fist to rest his swollen knuckles against the icy-cold pack.

"Maybe you should put that on your cheek," Sammy said, lifting a finger to point at Reaper's right cheek.

"Need my hands more than I need this face," Reaper said, his voice dead even. He was still pissed his brother cost him a huge chunk of change for the damages he'd caused at the bar.

Sammy grunted and placed his own bag against his left eye, which was swollen shut and beginning to blacken. They both sat in silence, until Sammy released a long, loud sigh. "Sorry about the bar bill. I'll pay you back."

Reaper shot him a glare. *Don't lie to me. Fuck, don't say anything.*

His brother glanced away. "Maybe I should head back to my place."

"Your bike's back at the bar, and you're still drunk." Reaper tipped his head from side to side to ease a knot forming in his neck. Talking to his brother always made him tense. "Why the hell did you pick a fight with McNally?"

"He took the first swing."

Leaning forward, Reaper shot him a glare. "You grabbed Danielle's ass. Do you think he was gonna let that slide?"

Sammy shrugged.

That gesture always fried Reaper's ass. Blood roared in his ears. "What?" he bit out. "You don't give a shit? Did you want him to kick your ass? What is it with you, lately?"

Sammy shoved back his chair. "Got a headache. Since you're not gonna take me back in town, I'll sleep on the couch."

Reaper watched as his brother pushed up from the table and turned to go. "I'll be up early. You want a ride, you be ready."

His brother didn't answer as he walked away.

For a few moments longer, Reaper sat in the kitchen, rolling his sore knuckles on the bag. He didn't like the direction his brother was heading, and he placed the blame squarely on Sammy's association with his bike club. The roadside bar didn't exactly attract the most upstanding citizens. They were a brawling, boozing bunch of ex-cons and misfits. As an ex-con himself, Sammy should have known better than keep that kind of company. Many of those losers worked at McNally's garage, Sammy included. The few times Reaper had dropped in, he hadn't liked the seedy atmosphere.

More than once, Reaper tried talking to Sammy about dropping his membership and finding another job, but Sammy remained stubborn. He didn't want his advice. Didn't need it, he'd said. The last time Reaper asked him about the club, they'd ended up fighting and hadn't spoken for a month.

If Sammy wasn't the only family he had, he might have let him learn some more hard lessons on his own. As the situation now stood, he was enabling his kid brother to continue his downward spiral. Tonight, he'd picked up the tab for the splintered furniture, broken glasses, and the six-foot mirror behind the bar.

Sighing, he lifted his hand and balled his fist, wincing at the tug of bruised muscles stretching over his knuckles. Well, hell. Tonight was clusterfuck. Tomorrow, he still wouldn't catch a break—not with an overeager ride-along asking questions and getting in his way. If he ignored her, he wondered how long she'd last.

His lips twitched. Yeah, he'd have Brian find the dirtiest, low-down target on their list and make sure she got muddied along the way. Nothing too violent, but something to make her reconsider hanging out with him for the rest of the week. Then maybe, he could talk his brother into riding shotgun and let him see what happened when dirtbags made stupid mistakes. Maybe he could rattle Sammy hard enough to help him see his current path would only lead to shit.

Reaper let out another deep sigh. With his adrenaline crashing, he was ready for bed. Feeling better about the next day's challenge, he tossed the thawing peas back into the freezer and smiled, which caused him to wince. Maybe he should have iced his cheek.

Nah. Maybe his face would make the author-*ess* think twice about sharing his SUV.

CHAPTER 2

Carly Wyatt arrived early at the Montana Bounty Hunters office in Bear Lodge. She would have been content to wait in her car until the appointed time, enjoying the view of the rugged Salish Mountains in the distance, but the office manager, Brian Cobb, appeared on the porch and waved her inside.

She hadn't really minded losing her "alone time." Brian was an interesting man, for more than the simple fact he wheeled around the office at breakneck speed. The loss of both of his legs wasn't slowing him down. Built lean—and maybe a little too skinny—he had a sharp edge to his cheeks and jaw, and a sparkle in his eyes. It wasn't hard to see that he loved his work.

After he poured her a cup of coffee, he invited her to sit beside him as he pulled up a database of available bounties. One by one, they clicked on the bench warrants. "Other than verifying with Fetch that he hasn't sent out any of his crew to round up these guys, we can pick and choose. We start with the highest-paying—usually for the most dangerous criminals, because judges don't like to make getting bail easy."

Not anything she didn't already know, but she was making mental notes about Brian, thinking he'd be a great character for the series she planned about a group of Rocky Mountain bounty hunters. "How'd you get into this line of work?" she asked, unable to still her curiosity.

A slight blush crept across his sharply etched cheeks. "A friend of mine, Jamie Burke, went to work for Fetch. She was pulled in to work on a case involving the FBI. A manhunt for a terrorist who escaped from jail—"

"You're talking about Mohammed Nazari? I read about that."

Brian nodded. "Anyway, I volunteered in the search team's command center. After the team captured Nazari, Fetch offered me a job. When he asked Reaper and Jamie to head up this office, I asked to come as well."

Impressed, she whistled. "Wow. Nazari was big news."

Brian snorted. "To hear the FBI tell it, they took down the bastard all by themselves."

Carly grinned, excited that she might get the inside scoop. "What was the real story?"

Brian smiled, but the moment he opened his mouth to continue the story, the office's front door slammed.

Carly jerked around her head to watch as a very tall, very muscled man approached. Dear Lord, Fetch had described him as a "big Swede", but a more apt description would have been a Viking. Or Thor, the god of thunder.

And Fetch hadn't mentioned how...arresting...his appearance was. Her heart fluttered, and her palms grew moist. Long blond hair was pulled back from his face, likely held in a ponytail. His face was bruised, which oddly only added to his rugged good looks of high cheekbones and a granite jaw. His lips pressed into a thin line, so she couldn't tell whether they were naturally thin. Didn't matter. His glacier-blue gaze pierced as it settled on her, and then swept over her body, before that razor-edged jaw tightened another notch.

Carly cleared her throat and pushed upright from her seat to move closer, her hand extended. "Carly Wyatt," she said. "You must be Reaper."

His gaze narrowed then dropped to her hand. With some reluctance, he reached to capture her hand.

Hers was swamped inside his large, hard grip. Again, her heartbeat soared. He'd make the perfect hero for her stories. While she'd planned to feature different members of the agency in each novel, now she reconsidered.

He still hadn't said a word. His gaze darted to the monitor and the list of bounties. He leaned past her, close enough she had to edge back to avoid them colliding. *Well, that's rude.*

He tapped a line on the screen. "That one."

His voice was deep and graveled, which sent a shiver down her spine. By his biting tone, he was already irritated.

"You do know today's his wedding." Brian's eyebrows rose. "Saw the notice in the paper."

Reaper's smile didn't reach his eyes. "Yeah, it's local. We won't have to go far. And we know exactly where he'll be. Print it." When he straightened, his gaze dropped to her, once again, scanning her body. His frown deepened.

She drew a sharp breath. Although she'd been warned about his "rough edges" and un-PC behavior, his perusal now bordered on insulting. What was his problem? She'd dressed appropriately in a long-sleeved, waffle-weave Henley shirt, her oldest, most comfortable Levis, and well-broken-in hiking boots. *Oh.*

His gaze centered on her holster.

"I have a permit." She hated the fact she sounded a little defensive...and breathless.

Beside her, Brian snorted. A smile tugged at the corners of his mouth.

"Don't care," Reaper said. "You won't need it."

She lifted her chin. "I'm qualified."

Reaper's hands fisted on his hips as he leaned over her.

She refused to back down—or even retreat an inch. Instead, she leaned back and met his scowl with one of her own. "I'm qualified. I've fir—"

"Still don't care. I'm not getting my ass shot when you get nervous."

The nerve. She narrowed her gaze. "If I shoot your ass, it won't be because I'm nervous."

Brian snorted, and his shoulders shook.

Both Reaper and Carly aimed dark frowns his way, which only made him choke with laughter. Brain reached for the warrant on the printer and handed it to Carly.

Reaper gave her one more look then turned on his heel, heading for the door.

"Better not let him get to his vehicle before you do," Brian said in an overloud whisper. "He might leave you behind."

She reached for her knapsack and her lined, flannel jacket then hurried after the tall man. The front door nearly slammed into her face, but she pushed through and scrambled behind him, heading straight to a big black SUV that hadn't been in the parking lot when she'd arrived. "Did I do something to piss you off?" she shouted at his back.

He didn't answer, circling to the driver's side and hitting the remote on his key chain. The lights blinked. The door locks snicked.

She grabbed the handle and tugged it upward, then quickly slid into the seat beside him, knowing if she'd hesitated a second, he would indeed have left her behind.

He paused to give her another ice-cold glare. "Seatbelt."

"Yeah...right." She pushed her carryall down on the floorboard and fumbled for her belt. Then she straightened, took a deep breath, and stared straight ahead as he hit the ignition button and worked the gears to back from the space and pull out of the parking lot.

Fifteen minutes later, they arrived at a church. Reaper parked across the street, behind a bush that overran the corner of its yard, for cover, and then killed the engine. Already, cars were in the parking lot beside the church, mostly delivery vans. A woman wheeled a cart laden with flowers up the ramp to the side of the double doors. Another woman with a clipboard stood there, talking into her cellphone.

Not willing to let his rudeness continue unchallenged, and because she had a job to do, she gathered her pride and turned in her seat toward Reaper. "If the florist is just setting up, we have a while to wait."

Reaper reached and tipped open a pocket above the rearview mirror. He plucked a pair of sunglasses from the pocket and slid them up his nose.

Again, she drew a deep breath. "How did you get into this line of work?"

Reaper hit a button beside his door latch, and his window rolled down.

Now, she knew he was deliberately ignoring her. "Are you still pissed about my Berretta? I can assure you—"

The quick turn of his head locked her throat. But she wasn't intimidated. Not really. His reactions were fascinating. And she was beginning to enjoy the way he communicated. His silence spoke volumes. Fingers itching, she bent to her pack and drew out a notebook and a pen. "That's okay," she said, her tone even. "You're already giving me more than I could have asked. You know, I'm thinking about patterning my hero after you. So, your attitude is all good."

Yes, she was teasing him. The way his shoulders

bunched, and his jaw tightened, almost made her smile. "Of course, I'll have to give him an *issue*. Something personal that he works out through the course of the story. Like maybe he's afraid of women. Maybe his mother didn't hug him enough when he was a kid—"

Reaper's fingers drummed on the steering wheel, and then they stretched and wrapped around it.

"When my heroine saves his ass, he'll realize he had nothing to fear..."

He shook his head. "Do you ever shut up?"

"I'm told I'm a great listener," she said with an innocent smile.

He issued a snort.

"Maybe he's a virgin."

"Fucking hell."

Carly couldn't help it. She snickered, and then had to press her lips together to keep from outright laughing. He was making this ribbing way too easy. "My heroine can be a Dominatrix...teach him how to embrace his submissive nature..." She didn't write that genre of books, but the thought did tantalize, now that she'd met her *hero*. "Once she has him bound, she can start his lessons—"

Reaper shot out a hand and mashed a finger against her lips. "Your hero isn't submissive," he bit out. She made a noise behind her smushed lips, but he only pushed harder. "The only lessons you need to be concerned about are those I'll teach you. *We* are on a stakeout. Which means *we* need to keep out an eye for our target. No distractions."

She frowned but gave a nod.

He removed his finger and turned to stare at the church.

With the pressure gone, she pouted her lips and stretched them. They felt a little swollen where the rough pad of his finger had pressed. Funny, her nipples tingled while she thought about what the scrape of those pads would feel like there. *No distractions, huh?*

REAPER RESISTED the urge to wipe his finger on his jeans. Anything to erase away the feel of her soft lips. He'd woken in a shitty mood that morning, one made shittier when he'd realized his brother hadn't slept on the couch. He'd walked back into town to get his bike.

Now, he had to put up with the jabber mouth beside him.

Didn't matter she was cute, with bee-stung lips and rounded cheeks, and a tiny chin he just wanted to cup and lift... A muscle near his eye jumped. The fact he'd noticed straight away how good-looking she was irritated the heck out of him. The moment he'd entered the office to see her cozied up beside Brian, he'd nearly tripped over his own two feet. What was Fetch thinking putting her with him? Number one, he'd already been put through the grinder getting used to riding with Jamie. That she'd proven herself capable was a miracle in his eyes. Number two, attractive women were distractions, and he needed all of his attention when he chased after dangerous targets. He'd gotten over his attraction to Jamie, and thankfully, she was off the market...but this woman?

He tried not to look her way again. Her brown eyes were large and round, brimming with humor at the moment—at his expense. Her silky brown hair was caught up in one of those messy buns that begged a man to loosen it. She wore a long-sleeved shirt that hugged her chest, which looked full and round, and made his fingertips tingle because he wanted nothing more than to ruck up her shirt and have a peek. That her waist was the perfect, well-indented "handle" for a man to grab when he made love to her—well, he better not think too long about that because he was already semi-hard. And he hadn't yet got a good look at her ass, but her legs? *Fuck.* They were long and nicely shaped. And again, his mind wandered to its predictable conclusion.

Reaper acknowledged he was a horn dog. Everyone who knew him was well aware of the fact. *What the hell, Fetch?*

Luckily, more cars arrived, pulling his attention from the lust-magnet sitting beside him.

"Looks like some of the guests are arriving," she whispered.

Like the folks outside could hear what they said inside his vehicle. The way she whispered let him know exactly what she'd sound like in the dark...in his bed. Her whisper was almost as sexy as her regular speaking voice, which was kind of musical, like the sexiest Blues. "Just don't talk."

"Again, did I do something to piss you off?"

She didn't sound angry with him, which he found perplexing. He'd never understand a woman's mind. No, she just sounded curious. Would she be as curious in bed? In his head, Reaper started counting. Anything to get his mind out of the gutter.

"So, what's the plan?"

Without taking his gaze from the cars entering the parking lot, he said, "The plan is that you sit tight while I tag the bastard."

"You're just waiting for him to step out of the car? What if he jumps back inside and tries to get away?"

Amateur. He took a deep breath. "I'll wait until he's inside and too many people he cares about are around him."

"That's the plan? You're waiting until they're saying their I do's, and then you'll stride down the aisle to take him into custody?"

Hell. He'd thought it a good plan until she'd said it out loud. "You got a better idea?"

She wrinkled her nose. "No, but why wreck their day? Catch them at the reception afterward."

"He drove drunk into a tree. I'd be doing his bride-to-be a favor."

She shrugged and turned her head, affecting she didn't care what he said, but he could tell she hadn't liked his words. "You write romances, don't you?"

Her chin lifted. "And if I do?"

"Makes sense," he mused, glad the shoe was on the other foot, now that he had something to poke and prod her about. "Bride's gonna help him walk the straight and narrow, right?" He lifted his chin toward the people ascending the church stairs. One or two faces looked familiar. "I'm guessin' groom's already got friends behind bars by the looks of all the tattoos and shaved heads."

"I have a tattoo, and I don't know a soul who's served time."

He almost barked a laugh. He had them all over his back, down his arms and across his chest. If she wasn't his responsibility this week, he might have liked giving her a peek. "Well, seeing as I've hauled a few of them off to jail before, I know that crew's not a bunch of boy scouts. If we don't take him when he steps out of his car, we might be looking down a barrel or two."

"We?"

The speculative note in her voice snapped his attention. He shook his head. "Me. Your ass is staying right here."

"I could follow at a distance."

"No."

A black limo pulled up in front of the church. The groom stepped out, wearing a tux and gripping his hands above his head like he'd just won a prize fight.

"That's our boy." Quickly, he let himself out of his Expedition and circled behind to open the back hatch. While keeping an eye out for the men gathered around the groom to give hugs and slaps on the back, he donned a Kevlar jacket, slid the clip with his badge onto his belt and placed his Glock in his holster. When he slammed down the door, he found his pain-in-the-ass companion standing beside him.

"Fetch said I could follow you through your day. I'm following you into that church."

"Lady—"

"Name's Carly, in case you forgot."

"Lady..." He again glanced at the church. The groom and his groomsmen were walking up the steps. "Don't get in my way. You stand way the heck back. Don't even let them know you're with me."

"I can do that," she said, her voice snippier now.

Angry now, he ran from behind the bush to the manicured hedgerow that faced the road. The groom's wedding party wouldn't see him coming up behind them.

When he was close enough, and all gazes were on the steps as the men climbed, he darted out of the hedgerow and ran for Winston Guidry.

In the distance, he heard a car's tires screech as it pulled up. He was almost within reach.

A door slammed open. "Winston, baby, run!"

Cussing, Reaper lunged for Winston just as he glanced over his shoulder.

Winston's gaze went to the woman in the white dress, and then swung back a second before Reaper grabbed the collar of his tux and swung him toward the ground.

Straddling the steps to cinch Winston's thighs to keep from getting kicked, Reaper slapped on the cuffs, glancing up just in time to see a blur of blue speed past him.

The bride tossed her bouquet at Carly's head then charged her like a linebacker. Both women went down, most of the action masked by voluminous white petticoats.

Winston stopped moving and lifted his head. "Damn, I'm gonna marry that girl."

His groomsmen swarmed around them, fists clenched.

"Man, this is fucked up."

"It's his wedding."

Winston lifted his head higher. "It's okay, baby, don't get yourself hurt."

The bride pushed up and flipped her veil behind her head. "You ain't supposed to look at me, jackass. It's bad luck."

"I'm already the luckiest man ever lived, Luann."

Reaper rolled his eyes and shot a glare at the men moving in closer. "Unless you want to join him in a jail cell, keep back. Winston here didn't make his court date. I have to take him in."

Carly rolled to her knees, giving the bride a wary glance, and rubbed her jaw. "What do you say, Reaper? Can we let these two say their vows before we bring him in?"

He gave her a baleful glance. Of all the stupid ideas... Then he saw the big red mark marring her pretty cheek. "What the hell, Carly?" he roared. "I told you to stay the hell back!"

"Doesn't sound like she follows order very well." Winston snickered. "We both have some strong women."

"She's not my woman." A muscle throbbed in his clenched jaw.

"Then why're you so pissed?"

Reaper dragged himself up from the steps then

reached down to grip Winston's arm and help him to his feet. "I'm doin' you both a favor."

Winston sniffled. "Man, she's the love of my life. We saved six months for this wedding."

For fuck's sake. The man was crying. Reaper shot a glance at Carly, whose mouth twitched. Was she laughing? He gave her a glare, which had her bending over and holding her stomach.

Damn, he knew she was already making mental notes for her damn book. But disheveled, and even with a big rosy bruise on her face, she was damn beautiful. "Fucking hell," he muttered.

CHAPTER 3

AFTER REPEATING the tale of the wedding fiasco twice to Brian, the luster was wearing off. Even the fact Reaper still muttered under his breath couldn't keep Carly from yawning.

WhenWinston had broken down in tears and his bride knelt in front of him, holding him while he leaned into her sturdy body, Reaper grudgingly agreed to let the wedding proceed.

Which meant Reaper and Carly joined the bridesmaids and groomsmen in the front of the church—Reaper to be ready to remove the cuffs so Winston could slide on the ring, and Carly to prevent Luann from attacking Reaper.

Sure, the tux was dusty and had a rip in one knee. Dark smudges marked the dress, and one of the ruffles on the skirt trailed behind the bride. Still, the wedding was strangely romantic, with the young couple standing close, tears in their eyes while they exchanged their vows.

Following the wedding kiss, Winston waited with his hands behind his back for Reaper to cuff him again, and then didn't offer a single complaint as he was walked down the aisle.

His friends and guests had stood and cheered.

Brian chuckled again. "Hey, Reap. You must be getting soft in your old age, letting them get hitched."

Jerking his head, Reaper grunted. "You got your paperwork. How about shutting your yap?"

Brian's grin widened, and he turned to Carly. "You've got a bruise to match Reaper's," he said, pointing at her cheek.

"Thanks for reminding me," she said, rubbing her sore face. "I don't think there's enough concealer in the world to hide this shiner."

Reaper cleared his throat.

She turned toward where Reaper stood and raised a brow in question.

Reaper frowned. "You got a bag of frozen peas to put on that cheek? It helps...uh, with the swelling."

His words were garbled, like they'd been dragged out into daylight. "No, I have a room at the Motel 6. No freezer. No peas."

"Uh, I have some at my place," he said, his gaze sliding away. "We could, um, pick up dinner. I'll drop you at the hotel after."

Brian's eyebrows shot upward, and he quickly turned his chair and began typing on his keyboard.

Carly's eyes widened, but she let her glance slide away. As reluctant as he appeared, she didn't want to give him a chance to rescind the invitation. Maybe she could figure out how to get on his good side if they spent a little time alone, without being "on the job."

Quickly, she bent to retrieve her rucksack. "Thanks. Um, that sounds good." *Great*. Now both of them sounded really enthusiastic about the idea of prolonging their time together. However, she realized she really was. Her heart skipped faster as she rose from her chair. "I'll see you tomorrow, Brian."

Following Reaper through the office and out the door, she couldn't help noticing the breadth of his shoulders or how sexy the long ponytail looked against his black leather jacket. Outside in the parking lot, she looked at her car. "I could follow you."

"No need. Back roads," he muttered, moving toward his vehicle. "You might get lost comin' back. Fetch'd have to send out search parties."

An exaggeration, she was sure, but now she was curious about why he'd made the offer in the first place. It wasn't like their conversations throughout the day had been leading to this awkward moment.

Keeping silent, she followed him to his SUV and climbed up into the cab. They drove through a fast-food window to get burgers, and then made the twenty-minute drive to his place in silence. Too dark to see her surroundings, she had impressions of dark roads and narrow gravel tracks. The SUV made several turns in the middle of the boonies until, at last, he pulled to a halt in front of a surprisingly spacious cabin. Two stories of log cabin with a wide front porch but without much of a yard. The forest came to the edge of a rough clearing.

When he opened his door, she did the same and followed him inside. A flick of the light switch had her blinking. She'd half-expected the walls to be rough-hewn logs as well, but the interior was a mixture of drywall and rock. The floors were a pretty golden oak. The space didn't hold an overabundance of furnishings, but what was there looked comfortable.

Reaper waved her toward a dark brown leather sofa.

Gratefully, she sank onto the cushion and continued to look around. The walls were painted a pale sage. A plain, nubby rug in eggplant sat beneath a rugged walnut coffee table. The colors surprised her. The attention to the decor—each piece in perfect synchrony but never matching. Fetch had made no mention of a wife, so Carly wondered if Reaper had a live-in girlfriend. The thought disappointed her. She bit back a sigh.

His footsteps returned. Reaper leaned over the sofa to extend a frozen bag of peas, already loosened.

Taking the cold bag, she held it to her cheek and winced.

"Keep it there for a while. The bruise won't hurt as bad."

"This the same bag you used on your cheek?" she asked.

He grunted and turned on his heel, returning with a tray holding plates with their burgers and chips. Condiments and knives sat to the side.

"Oh, thanks," she said, laying aside the bag to reach for her plate. "Didn't realize how hungry I was."

Taking his seat, he mumbled, "Should have packed some food for the stakeout. Didn't think to run into a shop."

"Was that almost an apology?" she teased. When she met his gaze, she blinked.

His gaze was narrowed but not in anger. His gaze was...assessing. At the intensity, she swallowed. "You always this quiet?"

"I talk."

"To girls?" she quipped.

He arched a brow. "To my partner. Friends."

She narrowed her eyes before she pushed her point again, "Not to girls?"

"No need," he said, taking a bite of his burger.

As she dug into her meal, she could well imagine what a date with Reaper would be like. A drink in a bar. His hand wrapping around his "date's" as he led the way to his car. No conversation, indeed. And she understood how a woman might fall in with that. The man was a rugged, well-built hunk. His surliness was its own sexy challenge. But that appeal wasn't why she was here.

"You write books."

At least he was speaking in three-word sentences. "I do. Romances, as you so cleverly surmised."

"Why bounty hunters?"

She understood what he was asking in his brusque way. "I've written cowboys, Navy SEALs, cops, and firefighters. I wanted something different. Heroes who operate a little outside the law. Men with rougher edges," she said, then pressed her lips together, because she'd just described him.

He grunted and took another bite of his burger. He chewed the bite twice and swallowed. "You handled yourself...all right...for someone who sits at a desk all day..."

She laughed.

He gave her a scowl. "What'd I say that's so damn funny?"

"I've only been writing full-time for about two years. Before that, I was in the Army."

He looked at the ceiling and drew a deep breath. "That where you met Fetch?"

Straightening, she gave him a grin and a mock salute. "Sergeant Wyatt, at your service." She waggled her eyebrows. "So, I do know how to hit what I aim at."

They finished their meal in silence.

A more relaxed silence. She couldn't help noticing the glances he darted her way every now and then. She liked that she'd surprised him. Between bites, she looked at him as well. And what she saw made her pulse ratchet up a few notches. Reaper's manners might be a little rough around the edges, and he didn't have a clue how to talk to a woman, but she rather liked those qualities. That he was built like a god—tall, broad, with muscles stretching his shirt and jeans—made her cheeks grow a little flushed. She cleared her throat. "I'm thinking Fetch likes to hire ex-military."

He nodded. "My partner, Jamie, and Brian served in his unit."

"And you...?"

"I was a marine," he bit out, his eyebrows lowering.

Sensing that was not a topic for discussion, she gave him a little smile. "I think I'll save the rest of my questions so we'll have something to talk about tomorrow."

"You finished?" he asked, glancing at her empty plate.

"Yeah." She glanced at her watch and noted the late hour. "I'll need that ride back to town."

"Need another bag of peas?"

His gruff voice rasped across her skin, and her face flushed hotter. *I need to get out of here. I couldn't stand him this morning, and now I'm wanting to jump his bones?* "No peas," she said breathlessly. "I just need some rest."

When she stood and bent to pick up her plate, he waved a hand. "I'll take care of that. Let's go."

Was he in a hurry to get rid of her? Her pride smarting, Carly grabbed her knapsack and followed him to the door. "You have a really nice place."

"It's a work in progress. You should see the upstairs..." He frowned and shot her a glance.

His expression was like he just realized the only way that might happen was if he invited her to bed. She couldn't help it; she laughed. "I promise, if I get a chance to see it, I won't judge." Then she pressed her lips together, because his eyes narrowed. Neither of them were thinking that "it" referred to his bedroom.

His lips twitched. "Sweetheart, if you see it, you'll be impressed."

Five minutes later, Reaper was still grinning. Carly's face had gone beet-red when they'd traded innuendos. And from the glances they'd exchanged, he knew she was as interested as he was to follow through on the flirtation. But he was afraid to make the first move in case he said the wrong thing.

She shifted in her seat, angling her body toward his. "Maybe we should just get it over with," she said, her voice a little high-pitched.

A pang of disappointment had him frowning. "You don't want to ride with me?"

She let out a loud breath. "I mean..." She drummed her fingers on the door beside her. "Maybe...we should just...*do it*."

The words were spoken so quickly, he wasn't sure he'd heard right. He aimed a glance her way, but he couldn't see her expression in the dark. His eyebrows shot upward. "Did you just say...?"

She blew out a breath and looked out the side window. "We'll both be more relaxed."

"You're asking me to fuck you?"

"Yeah." She nodded fast. "Let's fuck. We're adults. I'm...attracted. I think you are, too. We have to spend the next week together, and I can't imagine how the hell I'll keep my mind on the job when I—"

"Shut up a second, okay?" He shifted his position.

The way she talked—so quick and breathless—had his dick stirring. "Hell, lady, you always move this fast?"

She waved a hand. "Sorry. I shouldn't have blurted that. Forget I said it."

His blood pounded in his ears. "Not possible. I'm already a walking hard-on."

"Really?" Both eyebrows shot upward.

He gave her a stern frown. "Want to check?" he gritted out, a little indignant she was so quick to withdraw the offer.

A hand glided over his thigh and right between his legs.

"Motherfucker," he whispered before he gritted his teeth.

"Not the word I would use." She chewed her lip and bunched her eyebrows. "Didn't expect it to be so proportional." Her hand cupped him through his jeans and ran down his length and back up. "We'll need condoms. Jumbo-sized."

"Got 'em back at the house."

"I'll need clothes for the morning."

"I'll pull up outside your motel door. You got your key handy?"

"Only take a minute."

Feeling like a teenager getting his first feel of a girl's southern parts, he wasn't sure he'd last long enough to make the drive back. "Might have one in my wallet." He steered into the Motel 6 parking lot, his grip tight on the wheel.

"Room's around the left side. Second door."

So he goosed the gas, because he was getting nervous. Before he came to a halt, she'd opened the car door. He hit the button to kill the engine and yanked down his door handle. He was behind her, his hands on her hips before she finished opening her door.

Once he'd stepped all the way inside, he kicked the door shut then set her away from his body. "Get those clothes off."

"Yeah. Sure," she said, not turning, but her shirt went flying a second later. So did her bra.

Watching her toeing off her boots reminded him he'd better not leave her waiting. He dragged off his clothes, nearly toppling when he tried to pull feet from his boots at the same time he pushed down his pants.

At last, they were both nude. His gaze roamed her sturdy frame—a narrow waist, lush hips and ass. With his thumb and forefinger, he ringed the base of his cock and closed his eyes, willing his dick to relax a little. Otherwise, he'd shoot his wad the second she turned.

He heard rustling at his feet and peeked downward. Carly was on her knees, turning out his pockets. After she palmed his wallet, she flipped it open and went right to the space behind his ID.

When she pulled out the condom, she glanced up and waved it. "Got it!" Then her glance went to his dick. "Holy fuck," she said, eyes rounding. A little line appeared between her brows.

"I'll fit," he growled. "No changin' your mind now."

Smiling, she held up a finger. "Just a sec, okay?" She

moved closer and shifted onto her knees. Her hot breath gusted against him, and his cock jerked.

"Don't even think about it," he warned, his voice rasping. "I'm gonna blow."

"You keep holding what you're holding. I've never had something that big inside my mouth."

A laugh caught him by surprise. He liked how blunt she was. How honest—without sounding any less a lady. "Look, we fuck quick. Gather your things and check you out. We can take our time at my place."

Her gaze tilted upward.

"Swear to God," he whispered. "With your face that close to my dick..." He'd never seen anything sexier than her slitted eyes peering up at him, her mouth half-open.

"Okay," she whispered. She held out the condom. "My hands are shaking too hard."

He made quick work of the condom and lifted his chin toward the queen-size bed. "Sit on the edge and lie back."

Nibbling her lip, she shook her head. "I'm already wet."

His pulse ratcheted up. "And I'm still bigger than you've ever had. Do it."

She sat on the edge, her knees together, her breasts quivering with her ragged breasts.

He nearly groaned. Her breasts were on the generous side, round and rose-tipped. The tips were beaded, poking upward like they begged for a mouth to suck them like a straw.

He moved closer and went to his knees, then slid his

hands between her thighs and pressed to gently coax them open.

But they remained tightly closed.

He glanced at her face. Her eyes were wide, and her nostrils flared. Her pupils had nearly devoured the pretty whisky-brown irises. "Changing your mind?"

"You told me it was already too late," she said, her jaw tight.

"Do you want me to stop?" he asked slowly, thinking if she said yes, he might cry.

Instead of speaking, she reached out and tentatively placed her hands on his shoulders, then smoothed her palms down his upper arms. She squeezed as she went, and her gaze followed her motions shifting side to side. "You're in some kind of shape," she whispered.

The awed tone dried his throat. He flexed a bicep and watched her flinch. "Open your legs, Carly."

Her grip tightened. She closed her eyes and her lips formed an O. Slowly, she inched apart her thighs.

"Lie back," he said, softening his voice to coax her along.

Nodding, she let go of his arms and lowered to her elbows, then lay flat on the mattress.

"Not dissin' your tits, because they're fucking beautiful, but want to eat you out, sweetheart." He ran both hands over her thighs, savoring her smooth skin. "Have to make sure you're ready for me. You play with your tits."

Her nose wrinkled. "You must think I'm being silly. I'm the one who propositioned you. I asked for this, but now, I'm a little…"

He held still, wondering if he'd heard hesitancy in her voice. "You scared?"

"Fuck no!" She opened her eyes.

Her expression looked a little desperate. Reaper liked that look.

"I'm...shaking. Too excited."

"I can work with that." He smoothed his hands along her trembling inner thighs. "I like how fast this hit. It's not like I haven't seen a chick and had her bent over the seat of my Expedition five minutes later, but... I wouldn't have cared if she'd decided to back out. Last minute."

She wrinkled her nose. "You'd care if I did?"

He nodded. "My balls ache." He dropped his gaze to her pussy. Lord, she was bare. Her outer lips were a cool, pale pink. Her darker inner labia protruded from between them. His cock jerked. "I want inside that so bad my dick's ready to burst."

"Stop worrying about getting me there, Reaper." She cupped her breasts, splaying her fingers so the needy tips peeked between her fingers. Then she lifted her legs, toes pointing toward the ceiling, before she let them fall apart.

Her pretty lips parted, and he dove for them, sucking them into his mouth where he chewed and tugged and licked, until her head thrashed side to side. The taste of her, fresh and salty, exploded on his tongue.

Then he forked his fingers and pulled up her folds, exposing her reddened clit. With his other hand, he drove a single digit inside her and swirled, relieved to find her inner walls drenched. When he bent to suck her clit, he thrust another finger inside, then pushed in and out while she gasped and hissed, and her pussy clenched around his fingers.

"Damn, girl," he whispered and rubbed his stubbled chin around her sex, abrading her delicate flesh. He withdrew and gripped her waist. "Move up the bed." Only he didn't give her time to do it on her own. He crawled over her legs and used his thigh against her pussy to push her upward. When they were in the center of the bed, he hooked his arms beneath her knees to raise them and looked down between their bodies. "Put me inside you," he rasped.

Her hands shook, but she gripped him and rubbed the tip of his cock up and down her folds, wetting it thoroughly, before placing it at her opening. Then she raised her gaze to meet his.

Releasing her knees, he braced his hands on the mattress and eased inside, rocking forward and back, then giving a little side-to-side motion to work his way into her tight channel. He grimaced against the snug fit, worried because she felt so damn good and he wasn't sure he'd last long enough to please her. Concentrating hard, he gauged her comfort and arousal by her changing expressions.

Her eyes lost focus. Her mouth stayed open and rounded as her breathing grew more labored. Her breasts were hard, and she kept arching her back to rub the tips against his chest.

So fucking sexy, he wished he could contort his body to suck on them while he fucked her, but no way was he leaving her slick heat. She was tight and wet, and he could feel little rolling convulsions caressing his dick from inside her. Damn. For sure, he wasn't gonna last much longer. "Play with your clit, baby. I'm close."

She slid her hand between her legs, but reached past her clit to ring him with her fingers.

Her touch gave him goose bumps. He moved in and out, letting her feel how big he was.

Her mouth curved. "Think this is gonna work?" she whispered. "That we won't be...thinking about this...all day tomorrow?"

"I'll just have to wear your ass out tonight, girl."

"Not a girl," she said, pouting her mouth but narrowing her gaze. "Any *girl* ever tell you you're a chauvinist?"

"Yeah. Plenty." He gave her an unrepentant grin.

"Bet they did. Bet they didn't care so long as you fucked them like this."

"You like it?" He watched her face as he changed the angle of his strokes.

Her eyes rolled back. "God, yeah."

He lowered his body then slipped his hands under her ass and cradled their bodies closer, changing his strokes again, his thrusts shorter, sharper. "Your clit, baby," he ground out.

"Don't need it," she said, her voice thin.

To make sure she got what she needed, he ground against her with every upward stroke.

Her hands clawed at his back and dug into his ass. "Harder," she said, grunting now every time he hammered.

Suddenly, she went rigid, her head digging into the mattress, her lips baring her teeth. She cried out, her eyes widening as her orgasm shuddered through her body.

His signal he could concentrate now on his own pleasure. He clutched her ass and hammered faster, getting breathless and growling. When his balls clenched, he shouted and rocked, the ebb and flow slowing as his balls emptied.

How long he rested against her, he hadn't a clue. He became aware of her fingertips stroking along his spine, of her legs relaxing, releasing their fierce grip around his hips. When he raised his head, he stared down into her pink face. Realizing he'd broken fucking protocol, he grimaced. "Sorry."

Slowly, she raised her eyebrows. "For what?"

"For the fact I never kissed you."

Her lips twitched then stretched into a slow, sexy smile. "You've also never sucked my tits."

His body shook against hers. Then he opened his mouth to speak.

She placed a finger over his lips. "Shush," she said. "You weren't dissing my tits. I know. And my mouth is still right here."

"You're all right," he said, wishing he had a glibber tongue. She deserved someone who could shower her with pretty compliments.

"I'm better than all right," she said, cinching tight her inner muscles to give his cock a squeeze.

Groaning, he locked his gaze with hers. "You'll stay with me this week..."

"I like the way you don't even ask," she said, stroking his sides. "Not a rise in inflection or even a second of doubt in your tone."

"Glad one of us can speak."

She angled upward and kissed his cheek. "I've got plenty of words for both of us," she whispered in his ear. "An entire vocabulary of nasty ones."

He grinned and came up on his elbows, then looked down between their bodies. "My dick doesn't want to leave."

"I don't want to wake up staring at this ugly ceiling. I'd rather wake up staring down at you."

Reaper didn't need another nudge. He pulled free and rolled off the bed. "Get packed, woman. You're comin' home with me."

CHAPTER 4

THE NEXT MORNING, Reaper worked in the office with Carly seated beside him as he followed leads for his next hunt.

Brian gave them quizzical looks.

Likely the office manager was curious about Reaper's behavior, because he never hit the "soft" part of the job with so much enthusiasm. However, Reaper liked having Carly next to him and didn't mind her many questions. He even let her handle a couple of the calls being made to his target's former friends. So, maybe the fact they'd shared off-the-charts sex put him in a good mood. He wasn't proud.

Today, he was working on a more profitable case, having decided Carly wasn't a total liability to an investigation. Plus, Fetch had called, pretty much demanding he take the case. Dwayne Cummings, their target, was a three-time loser, whose bail had been set at a hefty $300,000. The timeline was running up on ninety days since Cummings had failed to show for his court date, which meant a friend of Fetch's in a bail bonds business in Great Falls, would be liable for the entire amount of the bond if they didn't find the bail-jumper soon.

Which translated into plenty of incentive to run him down. If he and Carly brought him in, the agency earned ten percent. Of course, flattery had also gone a long way.

"You're the best I've got, Reaper," Fetch said in his raspy, cajoling fashion. "And I know you're without your right hand for the next few days, so I'll send down Dag to help out. I want Cummings before A+ Bounty gets him. Jerry Owens bet me he'd get to him first. I don't want that bastard winning—or snagging that thirty grand."

Reaper had raised an eyebrow. Fetch wasn't a greedy man, so Reaper assumed Jerry had gotten under Fetch's skin. Maybe Fetch's agents in Kalispell had been beaten to the punch one too many times by A+'s agents. Reaper knew the feeling well.

So, Cummings it was. The dirtbag was facing trial for aggravated manslaughter for hitting a pedestrian while being chased by the cops for a speeding ticket. If convicted, Cummings wouldn't likely ever walk free again.

He glanced at Carly, who busily jotted notes. "You do know if we get close to this guy, you can't pull that same shit like yesterday."

Carly's mouth twitched. "Since it's unlikely he'll have a bride bent on beating you with her bouquet, I think I'll be okay hanging back." Staring at the computer screen at Cummings' mug shot, she wrinkled her nose. "Besides, this guy's scary."

Brian hung up his phone and tore off the page with his notes. "I have an address for his girlfriend. Cummings' mom gave her up. She's pretty pissed he skipped. Her house and a family hunting cabin were listed as security on the bond."

"Thank God," Reaper said, happy for an excuse to get away from the desk. He wasn't great at squeezing for information over the phone. Flexing a little muscle in person was more his style. "Let's ride."

Carly stuffed her notepad into her knapsack.

"Good luck." Brian held out the paper.

Reaper swiped it as he walked past. "Thanks, bro. You get anything else, text it."

"Dag should be pulling into the parking lot any minute. Sure you don't want to wait for him?"

Reaper shook his head. "We'll watch the girlfriend. See if she's alone before we knock on the front door. Any sign of our guy, I'll call in."

"Remember, Jamie said if she was needed, we can call. She'll bring Sky."

"Good to know. If Cummings is there, and looks like he's entrenched, I'll call. Otherwise, I'd just as soon leave Jamie and Sky to their wedding shit." He shuddered. "If I hear one more word about red velvet versus lemon cake, or she changes her mind again about the color of my damn cummerbund..."

Brian laughed. "She finally talk you into being one of her bridesmaids?"

Straightening, Reaper grunted. "I'm a bride's guy."

"Guess that sounds better than a bro-maid."

Carly's mouth stretched into a smile.

But he would not be swayed. Reaper shook his head, and then said mournfully, "What woman doesn't have a slew of girlfriends busting a gut to be a bridesmaid?"

"Well, I'm happy to stand up with her," Brian said, his gaze narrowing.

"She could have eloped." *And save me all this fuss and drama.*

"Sky put down his foot on that one."

"But why involve me? I already witnessed the proposal." Although he'd given his word, he'd just as soon sit in the audience

Brian shook his head. "Get out of here. Find the girlfriend. I'll send Dag along as soon as he shows up. Might also give Jamie a heads-up."

Reaper held open the door for Carly.

She arched a brow. "Yesterday, you were ready to let it slap me in the face."

The door shut, and Reaper halted, facing her. "Yesterday, I wasn't playing nice."

She moved closer and looked up into his face. "But, today, you are?"

He gave her a mock scowl. "Only if you don't get in my way and don't get yourself hurt again."

A smile playing across her lips, she walked her fingers up the middle of his chest. "And if I do get in your way?"

Reaper caught her fingers and gave them a squeeze.

"Then I might still play nice, but only because I want more."

"Think if you let me get away with shit, I'll be...nicer?"

Shrugging, he grunted. "Well...yeah. That's how it works with most women." Reaper would never admit to a living soul how much he enjoyed this banter. Or her reactions when he said something that pissed her off—like now.

She gave him a mean glare.

"Did I offend you?" he drawled.

"I think you offended all womankind." She rolled her eyes.

One corner of his mouth kicked up for a second, but then he wiped his expression of all humor. "Baby, I'm serious. We come up against Cummings, you stay in the car. He's on his third strike. If caught, he'll do hard time. From talking to his ex-wife, I learned he's got a hair-trigger temper, and he will draw on me."

Her gaze turned solemn. "All right. I promise to be useless."

LATER THAT MORNING, Carly watched as a black Dodge Challenger pulled up behind them. They were parked just down the street from Amanda Berthold's house in Whitefish, in front of a vacant house with a FOR SALE sign. So Carly knew they weren't about to be chewed out for sitting in front of anyone's property. Glancing in the rearview mirror, she watched as a tall, broad-shouldered man exited the Challenger and sauntered their way. "We've got company."

"I know." Reaper watched his side mirror.

The tall, well-built man pulled open the back passenger door and slid across the seat. His gaze went first to Carly, narrowing then roaming her face and upper chest, then moved to Reaper who was scowling. "Guess we're partners for this takedown," the stranger said, reaching over the front seat to hold out his hand.

Reaper shook it. "Looks like Fetch had to drag the bottom of the goddamn barrel."

Carly couldn't tell by his tone whether he was joking or this was some kind of male-bonding activity—or just two guys pissing on top of each other. "I'm Carly," she blurted. "Not his partner...obviously."

"Fetch said you'd be riding with Reap for the week— if he didn't scare you off sooner. Said you served in his unit in the desert."

"Ex-Army MP," she said, nodding.

His hand extended toward her, and she shook it, despite the deep frown Reaper gave her.

"He didn't say you'd be pretty."

Reaper huffed a breath. "We've had eyes on Berthold's house for over an hour." He jerked his thumb toward Amanda's house. "No movement. Her car's in the garage."

The newcomer smiled. "So, we have plenty of time to get to know each other. Name's Dagger, but all my friends call me Dag." His gaze slid back to Carly.

A sparkle lit his eyes when his gaze met hers. Had he

noted Reaper's disapproval? Did he think the big Swede was feeling a little possessive? Carly wasn't sure why Reaper didn't look happy. Might have had something to do with the fact Dag was one handsome man—like movie-star-handsome, with a chiseled jaw, dark brown hair, and green eyes—and a body like Dwayne Johnson's. "So, is anyone else wondering why Fetch only hires pretty men?"

While Dag sat back and laughed, Reaper rolled his eyes. "You don't call a guy 'pretty' unless he's wearing more makeup than you are," Reaper muttered.

Well, she wasn't wearing much—only enough to hide the dark circles under her eyes from lack of sleep, the bruise on her cheek, and the beard burn around her lips. The little bit of eye shadow and lipstick was just to keep her from looking completely dead today. Not her fault someone wouldn't leave her alone long enough to get her beauty rest.

"He's just pissed because I used to work for A+." Dag smiled, answering her unspoken question. "I scooped his bounties a couple of times."

"You honeyed up to Brown's wife to get his whereabouts," Reaper said, disgust in his tone. "And you gave Spearitt's mama chocolates."

"You use what you have, bro." Dag flashed his white smile.

Carly grinned. "I like this—and I can use it. A rivalry between two bounty hunters. Maybe a woman in the mix. A love triangle."

"You write porn?" Dag said with a waggle of his eyebrows.

She chuckled, thinking it was a good thing she was immune to his charm, but enjoying it nonetheless. "Of course not."

"Damn shame. I could help you with the research."

Reaper let out a deep breath. "You two quit sexually harassing each other. We got movement."

Carly glanced out the front window to see a woman exit the house, carrying a handbag. She assumed the woman was Amanda, since the mother told Brian the girlfriend was a bleach blonde, and this woman had used at least two bottles of peroxide to obtain that particular shade of straw.

Dag clapped the top of the seat. "I can keep an eye on the house for Cummings, if you two want to follow her."

"You do that," Reaper said, not looking back as Dag opened his door.

Dag gave her a wink then slammed the door and strolled back to his Challenger.

As soon as Amanda backed out of her driveway, Reaper tapped his ignition and pulled onto the street.

"Dag seems nice," she said, watching him from the corner of her eye.

He made a grumbly noise, then said, "I suppose he's nice enough."

"I noted a little tension between the two of you."

"Like he said. He used to play with the opposition."

"You don't seem like the kind of guy to hold a grudge."

"I'm not."

"Then…"

Reaper's glance cut her way. "I didn't want him sweet-talking you."

Pretty much what she'd thought all along. And the knowledge thrilled her. "You're not used to it, are you?" she murmured.

"What?"

"Feeling jealous."

He gripped the wheel tighter. "Got nothin' to be jealous about."

"That's okay," she said, smiling as she faced forward. "I'd feel a little insulted if I wasn't having so much fun at your expense. I'd never go for him, you know."

"Why not?" he ground out. "Women like his looks. And he can talk to them."

"Maybe most women would," she said, her heart beating faster. "But he's not a challenge. Not like you."

"Think you have me all figured out, do you?"

"Of course not. You catch me by surprise at every turn." She couldn't hold back a smile. "I like that."

His gaze turned toward her, and she looked away. So, maybe her cheeks were blushing. She'd never been this bold with a guy, but Reaper inspired her to tell it like was. She was straight-up attracted to the big guy. Even his surly moods and deadly glares couldn't put her off.

"She's headed for groceries." Reaper flicked his turn signal to follow.

"Maybe I could shadow her. I wouldn't stick out so

much." She leaned forward to watch the car. "I could see what she buys. Whether she's buying for two...?"

He pulled into the parking lot, claiming a space on the diagonal from Amanda's. "I'll keep watch on her car. Don't engage with her. Don't let her see you looking at her, you hear?"

She nodded quickly, having no intentions of drawing attention to herself. Not when Amanda's boyfriend was a seriously dangerous man. Letting herself out of the car, she removed her holster and set it on the seat.

Reaper frowned, but maybe he figured she was safer without it. Although Montana was an open carry state, some folks still got nervous around armed people in public places. Plus, she'd draw less attention.

His gaze narrowed. "Anything seems hinky, you get the hell out. Just act natural, and you'll be fine."

She nodded. "Of course. All I'm going to do is take a peek at her cart." Giving him a little salute, she headed toward the pneumatic doors. Once inside, she scanned the front of the store but found no sign of Amanda. *Where would I go first? Produce?* She glanced at the signs on the ceiling and made her way left—after snagging a small basket to carry on her arm.

Amanda was squeezing oranges when she spotted her.

Quickly, Carly discovered pretending to be inconspicuous was hard. She ducked around the corner of an aisle selling potato chips and crackers, placed a few items in her basket before turning the corner again, and discovered that Amanda had moved on. Although her heart pounded, she forced herself to walk sedately and glance at the vegetables as she made her way to the end of the aisle.

Now, Amanda pushed her cart down the beer and wine aisle.

Carly snagged the first bottle within reach and stuck it in her basket, and then watched as Amanda passed the light beers and went straight toward taller, full-bodied beers. Seeing as Amanda was probably a size twelve, and wanted to stay on the low side of double digits, Carly felt certain the beer was meant for a man.

Mission accomplished, she headed out of the store, but she forgot about the basket on her arm until a bell dinged beside the doors. Face reddening, she turned and dropped the basket at the nearest cashier stand. "Sorry. I forgot my wallet," she said with a weak smile and hurried outside, hoping security wasn't being called.

When she made it back to Reaper's car, she pretended complete confidence when she stepped up into the SUV.

His gaze raked her face. "What happened?"

"Nothing. I think she's definitely buying supplies for a man. She bought a case of tall, cheap beer."

"Why's your face red?"

The man was too observant. "Why don't you mind your own business?"

He grunted and returned his gaze to the store. "You set off that alarm?"

"It blared all the way out here?" She wrinkled her

nose and sank against her seat with a sigh. "I forgot I was carrying a basket full of crackers."

He chuckled. "It's hard actin' natural when you don't feel that way."

Frowning, she turned her head toward him. "I'd suck at this job."

"We all have our strengths." He raised his hands and curled his index fingers. "I suck at 'personal communications'."

"Did you just do air quotes?"

He wrinkled his nose. "Did I look ridiculous?"

"A little," she said, a grin stretching across her mouth.

A familiar figure appeared at the entrance and hurried toward her car.

"There's our girl," Reaper said under his breath. He started the engine then waited until Amanda was pulling abreast of their vehicle to snake his hand behind Carly's neck and pull her toward him for a brief kiss. "Been wanting to do that all day."

Breathless, she licked her lips. "So, that move wasn't to disguise our faces in case she saw us later, sitting outside her house?"

"That, too." With a self-satisfied smirk, he shoved the gearstick into drive.

As soon as they returned to their previous position diagonally across the street from Amanda's house, Dag let himself in the back passenger door. "You bored yet?" Dag asked. "This is the job. We spend more hours sitting on our asses, waiting to see our marks, than anything else. You going to write about that?"

Carly shrugged. "I can make a daylong stakeout take place in a sentence."

"So, you making me a hero in your story? I'd even pose for your cover." He turned his head side to side. "Which side do you think is my best?"

Carly couldn't help it—she laughed. She'd noted the sparkle in his eye and knew he was doing what he could to annoy Reaper. From the color creeping up Reaper's neck, his tactic was working.

Reaper let out an exasperated huff. "Seeing as you two have so much to talk about, I'm taking a nap." With that, he abruptly tilted back his seat, bumping against Dag who'd been sitting forward.

"Guess it's just you and me, babe," Dag said with a wink.

Might as well make the most of the opportunity. She reached into her knapsack for her notebook. "If you'll keep an eye on the house, I have some questions I'd love to ask."

Dag smiled and turned to gaze out the window.

Carly glanced at Reaper and blinked wide when she spotted him peeking at her. She gave him a subtle wink, just so he knew *she* knew who she was going home with. Then she turned to Dag. "So, tell me. Why bounty hunting?"

REAPER HADN'T INTENDED TO, but he actually fell

asleep, despite the easy conversation and laughter that filled his SUV. Regardless of his irritation with Dag, he'd liked listening to their conversation. Carly was clever. She'd managed to learn more about Dag than Reaper had known through three or four years of an association with the rival bounty hunter. She'd even discovered why he'd left A+.

"The owner's daughter took over. Started being a pain in the ass over expenses and wanted reports about how we found our fugitives. Too much damn paperwork for me."

Carly tilted her head. "She hot?"

Dag sputtered. "Hot? Nah. Well, if you like redheads with sticks up their as—, uh, asphalt." He shook his head.

Hmmm. Carly pursed her lips and scribbled.

His girl was hiding a smile. The next time he opened his eyes, the sky was dark outside. He straightened his seat and glanced at his watch. "Shit. I've been out for two hours?"

"Yeah, Sleeping Beauty," Dag said. "Me and Carly are tight now."

"Besties." Carly grinned, her teeth flashing white in the dark.

"It's time we scope out the house. Find our probable cause." And get this the hell over so he could get Carly back to his place. He turned in his seat and narrowed his gaze. "You stay put," he said, his voice firm.

"Give me an ear piece so I can hear what's going on?" she asked.

"Yeah. Got Brian on speed dial?"

"I do. Anything gets 'hinky'—I'll give him a call."

He liked how he was rubbing off on her. Hell, he'd like to rub himself off all over her. Leaning toward her, and ignoring their audience, he gave her quick kiss.

"I knew it," Dag muttered.

CHAPTER 5

Dag and Reaper moved to the back of Reaper's SUV. Reaper opened the back gate and unzipped his duffel with his "go" gear. He pulled out a Kevlar vest and tossed a spare to Dag. Then he clipped his badge to the slot on the front of his vest and picked up the shotgun with the orange stock—his beanbag gun. He'd prefer using it to take down Cummings than fire a bullet with the Glock strapped to his side. "You ready?" he said, giving Dag a charged glance.

Dag patted a hand on his Glock and nodded.

Reaper pulled out a case with the earpieces and handed one to Dag, flipped the switch on another and put it in his ear. Lastly, he moved around to Carly's window.

She rolled it down and held out her hand.

"Know how to use it?"

Shaking her head, she swiped it off his palm and flipped the switch.

After she placed it in her ear, Reaper tapped her door and headed toward Amanda Berthold's house.

He signaled with his hand which direction he'd take. Dag moved the opposite way. Reaper liked that he didn't have to explain himself. Dag was seasoned, and he wasn't as worried about the other agent getting his ass hurt—not like he was every time he got into a sticky situation with Jamie. Jamie, he cared about.

He moved closer to the house, sliding under a window, then popped up to look between the slats of the blinds to peer inside a living room. The TV blared, set to some hunting channel, but no one was in the room.

Ducking downward, he moved farther along the one-story, box-shaped house. He paused beneath an ice block window, took a breath, and eased upward. The bathroom was dark; no blurred figures inside. Again, he sank and moved, bent at the waist, to the next window.

This time, he hit pay dirt. Even before he looked inside, he knew the room was occupied. The unmistakable sounds of sex—moans, groans, wet slaps—came muffled through the glass. In between the break in the curtains, he observed two figures, moving in the center of the bed. From the back, the man had the same greasy brown, shoulder-length hair as Cummings' mug shot. "Think we have our guy," he whispered. "In the back bedroom."

"All clear, my side of the house," Dag said, "Coming your way."

A few seconds later, Dag crouched down beneath the bedroom window.

While Reaper kept watch, Dag bobbed up then down, taking a peek. "Almost seems unfair," he said, his teeth flashing in the dark. "Might be the last time he gets some."

"Ah, he'll get plenty where he's going."

They traded grins, knowing Carly was listening in and likely rolling her eyes.

"We sure that's our dude?" Dag asked.

Reaper bumped up again, just in time to see Cummings standing beside the bed now, facing the window, while Amanda perched on the edge on her hands and knees. Her large tits jiggled as Cummings pounded her from behind.

"It's our guy all right," Reaper said, grimacing. "I'll take the front door. You watch the rear."

"Think we should call in back-up?"

Reaper shook his head. "He's not thinking with his big brain. I'll pick the lock. They're makin' enough noise they won't hear a thing."

The two men parted, and Reaper headed toward the front door. He ducked down beside the door knob, pulled out his lock pick kit, and quickly opened the door, grateful for the fact Amanda hadn't turned the deadbolt above the doorknob. "I'm in," he whispered before moving stealthily through the living room and into the corridor leading to the bedroom. When he stood in the doorway, he raised his shotgun. "Dwayne Cummings, Fugitive Recovery Agent! Raise your hands above your head."

Amanda squealed.

Groaning, Cummings darted his gaze to the gun on the bedside table.

Reaper stepped deeper into the room. "Don't even think about it, asshole." A second later, he heard the crash of the back door and footsteps moving quickly in his direction.

"Right behind you, Reaper." Dag edged inside around him and stepped toward the weapon.

"Dwayne, you can, um, pull out now," Reaper muttered.

CARLY STOOD at the edge of the lawn, wishing she could go inside the house and see what was happening.

That last remark from Reaper had her lips twitching, because she'd heard enough of the sounds echoing through the earpiece to know they'd caught Cummings with his pants down.

That scenario has to go in my book!

Too curious to wait to hear about it later, she moved to the side of the house and peeked into the living room window. In her ear, she heard cussing and Amanda crying, and then the rustling of clothes.

"I need shoes," a male voice said.

"Be glad I'm giving you pants, asshole," Reaper said in a mean voice.

"Found his shoes," Dag said. "Amanda, will you put them on?" Dag asked, his tone gentler.

Another minute passed, and then she saw Cummings

enter the living room, his hands behind his back and Reaper gripping his upper arm to move him forward.

Dag followed with Amanda beside him in a purple housecoat, her hair a mess, and her makeup running down her face.

When Reaper was at the front door, Carly realized she'd never make it back to the car without him noticing she wasn't inside. Frozen, she waited, undecided what to do next. The three men exited, crossing the yard just feet from her position, but then she noticed Amanda moving back into the living room. The woman made a beeline to a closet and pulled out a bat.

Carly sucked in a sharp breath and felt for her handgun. Deciding she didn't want to kill the woman, she reached into her knapsack. Then skirting the house, she hung back at the edge of the porch and waited.

A second later, Amanda ran out of the house, the bat held high above her head, and headed straight for the men.

Taking a deep, calming breath, Carly raised her weapon and fired.

Amanda gasped. A buzzing sounded, and then she dropped like a rock to the ground, her body jerking as electricity ran through her.

"What the fuck?" Reaper roared.

Carly walked calmly toward Amanda's body and plucked the dart-like electrodes off of Amanda's backside. Then she kicked away the baseball bat before glancing up at Reaper.

Even in the yellow light cast by the streetlamp, she could tell his face was mottled with fury.

Dag began to laugh.

Cummings cursed.

Reaper stood still, his body vibrating with anger.

"Oops," she said. "I know I was supposed to stay in the car..." She held up her cellphone. "I'll just call Brian to let him know we'll need a local deputy to pick her up." Turning her back, she quickly made the call then went back to Amanda's porch to pick up her knapsack, which she'd dropped in her excitement.

Amanda now sat on the ground, crying. "Dwayne, I tried."

Cummings snorted. "Stupid bitch."

Amanda cried harder as Reaper jerked away her boyfriend and pushed him toward the SUV.

In the distance, Carly heard sirens.

Dag called out, "Catch!"

She caught the keys he threw then frowned, not understanding.

"We have to get this guy to lockup." He jerked his head toward the captured man. "You can talk to the cops about Amanda. You'll need wheels. See you back at the agency."

A patrol car with its lights flashing pulled into Amanda's driveway. Another pulled in beside Reaper's vehicle. Knowing this discussion would take a while, Carly sighed and faced the deputy striding toward her. She held her stun gun upside down by the grip. "Evening, deputy."

"She fucking shot me in the ass," Amanda screamed, pointing at Carly. "Arrest her!"

Carly kicked the bat. "I was just protecting my guys."

"You a bounty hunter?"

"Nope," she said in a small voice, because the deputy's expression was deadpan—not a hint of humanity in his hard glare. Her stomach churned. "I'm a writer."

The deputy shook his head. "Ma'am, I'm gonna have to take both of you in to get this sorted out. Would you turn around and place your hands behind your back?"

Early the next morning, Carly sat beside Brian in his van as he drove back to Amanda's house so she could pick up Dag's car. He hadn't said a word since she'd been released. No charges had been filed against her. Amanda, however, faced attempted assault charges. She'd be spending the night in the Whitefish City Jail until morning, when she'd either be bonded out or sent to the Flathead County Detention Center.

Either way, she wouldn't be seeing Dwayne for a while. He was on his way to Great Falls, more than four hours away, accompanied by Reaper and Dag.

Carly blew out a deep breath.

"So, how's this research gig working out for you?" Brian asked, his tone nonchalant.

Her shoulders sank. "I think Reaper's pissed. He's

probably done with me. I disobeyed his instructions and put myself in harm's way."

"I don't know how done he is with you," Brian said, giving her a sideways glance. "He called me right after he hit the road for Great Falls. Told me to bail out your ass then give you the spare house key. Said you're to sit your ass tight there until he gets home. Pardon my French—those were his words."

Carly pursed her lips, fighting a smile. It was...inappropriate...to smile, given that she knew he was mad enough he might decide she needed to learn a lesson or two.

However, she couldn't feel anything but relief since he wasn't kicking her straight to the door. Maybe he intended to after reading her the riot act, but she figured she had ways to affect his decision.

"So, you tased Cummings' girlfriend?" Brian said, his teeth gleaming in the light from the dashboard.

"She was going after Reaper and Dag with a bat. What the hell was I supposed to do?"

He chuckled. "Better work on your delivery. You sound way too defensive."

ALL THE LIGHTS except the front porch light were out when Reaper arrived home early the next morning. He was hungry and dead tired after hours behind the wheel, listening to Dag's constant chatter—but first things first. He had a bone to chew with a certain brunette.

As quietly as he could manage, he entered the

bedroom, dropped his jacket and his holster onto the arm chair just inside the door, and then he flicked on the overhead light.

He blinked as he beheld the sight of Carly, lying nude in the center of his bed, the sheets covering her hips, but her lovely breasts bare. Another hunger rose inside him, pumping blood into his groin. He'd delay the ass-chewing she'd earned until after he'd had himself a piece of her pretty ass.

He turned off the light, stripped in record time, cloaked his cock, then strode to the bed and slipped in beside her. Moonlight filtered through the blinds, enough to display her creamy skin. She smelled fresh. He ought to shower as well, but he was too angry and horny. The time had come for them to get a few things straight—after he'd had his piece.

Carly awoke with a gasp when a large, heavy frame settled atop her body, trapping her against the mattress. Her body tensed. "Reaper?"

"Carly, we're gonna talk."

Immediately, she relaxed. "This how you hold all your conversations?" she asked, smiling in the darkness. She'd figured he could be distracted if she flashed a bit of skin when he first walked into the bedroom. By the size of the erection lying against her closed legs, she'd been right. "This...discussion would work better if you let me move my legs."

"This isn't about you. Not yet. It's about me. You

scared me half to death. I'm angry, hungry, horny as shit, and I'm gonna fuck you—then we'll talk."

Her eyes rounding, she gave him a swift nod. She was okay with the fucking part. Maybe an orgasm would sweeten his mood. She cleared her throat. "Still might be easier if you let me open my legs," she mumbled.

He blew out a breath and glared. "Hope you're already wet."

That was all the warning she got.

He rolled off her, then flipped over her body, and gripped her hips to raise them.

She scrambled to her knees, but he was inside her before she could raise up on her arms. The quick thrust pushed the air from her lungs. Then she scrunched the sheets in her fists and held on for dear life as he thrust swiftly.

She was wet. And more liquid engulfed her channel as he hammered. The first internal tremors flickered, and she tightened her muscles, squeezing around his big, thick cock. "Reaper!" she cried out, and let her back sink, needing him deeper, harder.

His groin and lower belly slammed against her ass. His fingers dug into the sides of her hips, holding her still as he moved faster and faster.

When he slammed one last time and held still, she groaned. She'd almost joined him. Leaning on one hand, she reached the other between her legs to take care of herself, but he pulled free and flipped her again. This time, when he came down on top of her, trapping her legs, she knew he'd deliberately withheld her pleasure.

She pouted her mouth and watched warily as he went to his elbows.

"What part of 'sit tight' didn't you understand, Carly?" he asked.

His voice sounded menacing in its softness. She shivered, discovering she liked his change of tone. Hell, gruff, growling, gently menacing—every one of his tones turned her on. That fact wasn't fair. "I had to see. Besides, I saved you from getting your skull crushed."

"I heard the screen door crash. I knew she was coming." His arms bunched. "I didn't need your damn help."

"Oh." She released a sigh, which rubbed her nipples against his chest, and once again, she was there, needing what Reaper could give her—if he'd just get over his crankiness. "I'm sorry," she said, thinking those words ought to do it.

Slowly, he shook his head. "Sorry doesn't cut it." Again, he rolled away, this time to sit on the edge of the bed.

Was this the part where he cut her loose and told her to find another hunter to annoy? Her stomach knotted because she'd hate that. Swallowing her pride, she pushed up on an elbow and reached to run her fingertips along his side. "What can I do to make this right?" she whispered.

His head angled toward her. His gaze was hard when it locked with hers. He patted his thigh. Twice.

Her eyebrows shot up. Did he mean...?

"Come here, Carly."

He was going to spank her! Seriously? Part of her ego bristled that this solution was the one he'd reached. He was going to treat her like a disobedient child. Another part noted that his cock was rising again...

So, biting her bottom lip, she crawled toward him until she knelt beside him.

His gaze swung forward. He barely breathed.

The telltale jerk of his cock lessened her humiliation. Slowly, with her lips pouting and her brows drawn together in the fiercest frown she could manage, she bent and crawled over his lap, lowering to rest her belly on his muscled thighs.

She felt his hardness against her hip and took heart from the fact this act was turning him on just as much as it was her. Not that she was into punishment. But the thought of what their bodies looked like, right this minute, sent another rush of liquid to drench her sex.

One hard hand settled at the small of her back and pressed down. The other he laid against her right ass cheek.

Carly rested on her elbows, just high enough to rub her nipples on the bedding, because she was aroused and growing more so by the second. "So, will you get this over with?" she asked, her voice husky.

"Don't think I take any joy...?" he said, his voice sounding like he was strangling.

"This how you trained Jamie?" she asked, acid in her tone. A hard smack landed, and she gasped.

"I don't fuck Jamie. Never did." He slapped her

again. "When bad shit happened, I kept it together, but this...you..." He slapped her again.

Fiery aches radiated from where he'd hit. "Ouch!" she said, contorting her upper body to give him a good scowl. "Remember, I have to sit on this ass."

"Maybe you'll think twice," he growled and smacked her again.

Only this time, his hand landed in the center. A moist slap. His breath hitched.

Carly held still, squeezing her eyes shut because the heat and pressure from his slap sent a wave of pleasure straight to her core.

"Dammit."

The roughness of his voice had her biting her lower lip. "You can stop," she said, her voice trembling.

The hand on her lower back lifted, and she scooted back, pressing her hands on his thighs to raise herself. With her breast pressing against his shoulder, she bent toward him to rest the hot side of her face against his cheek. "Reaper?" she whispered.

"Dammit." He gripped her arm and pulled her over him, waiting as she straddled his thighs.

Without thinking, she acted on instinct and gripped his cock, placed it at her center and sank on it, taking him all the way inside and settling against his heaving chest. When his arms came around her, she hiccupped. *Who is this woman?* She wasn't weepy. Wasn't given to tears, but she was so turned on, so desperate for his hands to caress her tenderly, she quivered against him. Waiting...

Reaper stroked his hands down her back then cupped

her buttocks. "Take what you need, sweetheart," he whispered.

What she needed? Confusion swirled inside her. She didn't need a man. Hadn't wanted anyone in her life—on a permanent basis, anyway. But being with him was like being in the center of a whirlwind. Her emotions were tugged in every direction.

She was wildly attracted, and she liked his terse intensity. Loved his sense of humor, when he let her see it. And when he made love to her? *Holy shit.*

Through struggling with what was happening inside her, she gripped his shoulders and pushed back, just far enough she could see into his face and lock with his gaze. Then firming her chin, she raised and lowered, aided by his strong hands, taking him in slow inches, until she couldn't breathe. She couldn't stop shaking. "Reaper?"

He didn't answer, just stood with her wrapped around him and moved toward the wall. Then he fucked her against it, grinding deep, shoving her up and down his cock, until they were both sweaty and hot, and her moans filled the room.

She'd never been loved this way. Full-on. Rough. "Damn, this is good," she said between clenched teeth, because she was riding toward the peak.

"Come, baby. Come quick. My legs are starting to shake," he muttered.

She laughed and rubbed her breasts against his hairy chest, her legs working up and down against his sides as he burrowed and thrust, until, at last, she screamed.

REAPER HELD her while she quieted, her whimpers leaking away on shattered breaths. He'd never seen anything like it—her face red, sweat dotting her forehead. He'd never seen anything quite so beautiful as Carly when she came.

Not that he was ready to express those sentiments. Instead, he held her, braced against the wall until she rolled her head toward his and kissed his cheek then his jaw.

His mouth quirked upward on one side as he mused he was lucky she was peppering him with kisses rather than punches for what he'd done. Something told him Carly wasn't into spankings and bondage, that she'd been as shocked as he was when he'd discovered her becoming aroused by his hand heating her bottom.

"Gonna move," he said brusquely. "Hold on." Then he walked, stiffening his legs against the weakness in his knees. When he reached the bed, he crawled up on one hand and both knees, his other hand cupping her ass to keep her body close. He wasn't pulling out any time soon. At the center of the bed, he rolled to his back and urged her with his hands to rest atop his body.

She yawned and moved her legs alongside his.

He slid a hand along her thigh and pushed them together, to trap his cock inside her heat. "Stay like that."

She nuzzled his chest and sighed. "I was afraid you'd send me packing."

"I considered it," he said truthfully. For about five seconds, until Dag laughed himself silly after he'd stated his intentions. Didn't take that jackass pointing out the fact he was only mad because she'd scared him.

"Can I still ride with you?"

"You already are," he quipped, a smile tugging at his mouth.

She pinched his side. "You know what I mean."

He let out a deep breath. "Yeah." He rubbed her ass, earning a very satisfying hiss. Her skin was hot. She wouldn't soon forget the lesson.

"I've never been treated like that," she whispered. "Not sure I liked it."

"You liked it, all right, but I get what you're saying. Spanking's not my thing either, baby."

Carly raised her head. "I like it when you call me that."

Telling her not to read too much into the endearment was on the tip of his tongue—as was his habit with previous girlfriends. But he kept silent. Carly wasn't one of his easy lays. Hell, nothing was easy about the woman, other than the sleepy, sexy look she wore right now. "You get charges?" he asked.

A shake of her head was followed by a rueful smile. "The deputy gave me a tongue-lashing about letting the professionals do their jobs."

He grunted, happy he wasn't the only one telling her she had no place in that takedown. "My work can be dangerous. Cummings could just have easily gone for his weapon. Or Amanda could have decided that a revolver would work better than a bat."

"I know." She wrinkled her nose. "But I couldn't let her hurt you. Or Dag."

"If you'd been in the car…"

"Yeah, yeah. I never would have been tempted to save you." She frowned. "You do remember I'm an ex-MP. I've had defensive training."

He stroked her back. "Have you ever had to use it?"

Her lips firmed. "No. I was strictly a jailer who watched prisoners. I never left the Green Zone."

"My partner, Jamie, saw real action. She can handle herself. Took me a while to trust her. With you…" He shook his head. "You will drive me to a heart attack."

She leaned to the side and rubbed a finger over one of his nipples. "Only thing I want to drive is you…crazy, that is."

This time, he yawned. He caught the finger playing on his chest. "Maybe when I wake up?"

"I'll be here." She gave a little wiggle of her hips, which tugged on his cock. "Doesn't look like I'm going anywhere…"

CHAPTER 6

They rose in the early afternoon and quickly showered, doing their best not to touch, because they were starving. But the no touching thing proved impossible, leading to plenty of splashing. After they dried the floor outside the shower stall, they dressed and headed into Bear Lodge.

Although her backside stung, Carly didn't dare grimace as she shifted on her chair. No way would she give him the satisfaction of knowing she felt a single ache. Today, she wasn't showing him any vulnerabilities, because she was worried she'd come off as a little too "needy" the night before. She didn't figure Reaper was in to clingy women, so she'd play it cool. Friendly, but not too familiar. No using excuses to cuddle against his side while he drove. She'd dish sarcasm when he gave it. Today, she'd be a buddy—one he'd hopefully want to fuck again when they returned to his cabin.

Because being in his bed wasn't something she'd ever

get enough of. Delicious aches, not on her ass, reminded her just how thoroughly and deliciously his big body and hard hands could pleasure her.

They ate in the cafe on Main Street, seated opposite each other in a red vinyl booth. She knew the looks they got. The women gave him sly, sideways glances before their glances flicked over her. Then they sniffed. She wasn't anywhere in his league, but she did get some curious and appreciative glances from the men, which went a long way toward mollifying her pride. A few frowned at the matching, fading bruises on their cheeks.

After they finished their breakfast and exited the cafe, he reached for her hand.

She was so surprised by the gesture she nearly jerked away. She'd never figured him for a hand-holding kind of guy. Turning her head, she hid a pleased blush. *Lord, now I feel like a teenager on my first date.*

"If you don't mind, I need to make a stop before we head back," he said, without looking her way.

"That's fine. I don't mind the walk." Anything to prolong the pleasant sensations radiating up her arm to her chest.

They walked two blocks to a corner garage. A row of Harley Davidson motorcycles formed a line at the side of the building in the employee parking area. Her curiosity piqued, she barely noticed when he let go of her hand and pushed through the shop door. He nodded to the man standing behind the counter—a rough-looking, rather skinny dude with his hair caught up in a rubber band. Tattoos ran across the tops of his fingers and up his arms.

They passed through the storefront and into the garage area. Reaper's head turned side to side, until he locked on one man bent over the open hood of an old Buick. "Sammy," he called out.

Sammy's head turned his way, and Carly's feet slowed. Sammy had to be related to Reaper. Same blonde hair, only darker and dirtier looking. Scruff on his cheeks and chin obscured what she knew had to be an equally strong jaw. The blue eyes, however, were the biggest giveaway. They were the same intense, arctic blue.

Sammy's brows lowered. "Hey, bro, what are you doing here?" His gaze darted around the garage.

Brother. Carly followed his nervous glance and noted the other mechanics working in pits or leaning over lifted vehicle hoods watched the byplay between the brothers. What was going on here?

"Just checking in," Reaper said, his mouth turning downward at the corners." You didn't answer any of my calls. Your phone broke?"

"Nah." Sammy turned away to flip a wrench around a nut on the car battery.

Carly was surprised by his disrespect. More surprised when Reaper simply sighed rather than reaching out to pull him around.

"Look," Reaper said, lowering his voice. "Call now and then. And if you need anything, you know I'm right here."

Sammy glanced over his shoulder and gave a casual

nod. "Sure." Then he turned back to the battery, but his hands didn't move.

Reaper dragged a hand through his hair. "See ya, Sammy."

Sammy didn't respond.

Carly followed on Reaper's heels as he turned and walked out of the open bay, his stride stretching too long for her to keep up, so she didn't try. She glanced back and spotted Sammy watching his brother stomp away, a look in his eyes she couldn't quite name.

Farther down the way they'd come, Reaper halted and turned, his troubled gaze following her process. "Sorry I didn't introduce you," he said in a surly tone.

"I sensed you two aren't on the best of terms," she replied, careful to keep her tone neutral and her expression impassive.

"Don't want to talk about it," he bit out. Then his mouth twisted. "Look, you want to stop by the office? See what's up?" His head jerked to the right. "Or would you like to take a drive into the mountains?"

Liking the idea of more time alone with the big guy, she said, "I don't think Brian's expecting us. You were out pretty late."

He flashed a grin. "Can you walk in those boots?"

After stopping for supplies, they drove to Lone Pine State Park and hiked trails all afternoon with stunning views of Flathead Lake, the Jewel Basin, and Big

Mountain. Late afternoon, they stopped at a park bench and ate their early dinner, not talking much.

Holding up an apple, she said, "You surprise me."

His head angled her way. His eyes narrowed and a small smile curved his mouth. "How so? Didn't think I could walk?"

She chuckled. "No, but I didn't think you'd like...this." She waved the apple toward their amazing view. "I figured you'd be more at home on dirt bike runs or maybe hunting along some log trail."

"Not taking a date on a hike in a safe place?" he asked, squinting.

That intense look made her stomach tighten. "Yeah."

"I haven't been out here in years," he said, looking away. "My folks used to bring me and my brother to the park. We'd pack a tent and set up at one of the campsites. We'd hike the trails or head down to the lake to fish..."

She didn't want to ask, but she'd noted the way his voice changed, getting a little rougher, when he mentioned his parents. "Are your parents gone?" she asked quietly.

"Yeah," he said, still facing away. "When I was twenty. Left me a little money. Left me my brother to take care of."

"A lot of responsibility for a young man," she murmured.

"Well, I failed." He shrugged. "I joined the Marines. An aunt took in my brother, and I sent him money and things. I didn't visit often enough. He got in with a rough crowd." His throat worked around a big swallow. "Wound up doing time."

Her hand moved several inches toward his face before she pulled it back. "I'm sorry."

"Not as sorry as I am. I don't know how to bring him back."

She took a bite of her apple and sat back as she chewed, letting the silence fill in the space. "That garage another rough crowd?"

His mouth thinned as he met her glance. "Just rumors. But I don't think the only service they provide is car and bike repairs."

Sensing from the way his fingers drummed his knees that he was getting restless with the subject, she said, "My parents never wanted me to join the Army. They wanted me to go to college and follow my sister's footsteps. Bev's a lawyer." Carly screwed up her face like that was the worst fate that could befall her.

Reaper chuckled. "Yeah, I can't see you as a lawyer, but I'm surprised you didn't want to go to college. You're plenty smart."

"The thought of four or more years of school nearly killed me. I joined the Army—and didn't tell my family until I had to ship out."

His eyebrows rose. "Seriously?"

She shrugged, feeling a little guilty. "Yeah. Saved my eardrums."

He gave her an assessing glance. "So...Army. No college. You seem to do all right. They're not happy about that?"

Shaking her head, she wrinkled her nose. "I'm not rich like my sister."

"Starving artist?"

"I do better than that, but nothing that will impress Dr. Dad."

"Ah," he said, nodding.

"Uh-huh, and what's worse, in their eyes, is that I'm not writing some bestseller. I'm just happy to do what I do. Find a story to tell..." She looked away, because her reason sounded a little foolish.

"I don't think you're foolish, Carly." His hand reached for hers, and he stood then pulled her upright. His gaze went to the sky. "We better head back, or we'll be using flashlights. Wouldn't want to meet a bear in the dark."

They headed down the trail. "I liked today." She flashed him a smile.

"Me, too. Being here's kind of restful up here."

She gave him a flirty, sideways glance from under her eyelashes. "How long to get back to your place?"

He tugged her hand. "Not long if you don't mind jogging a bit."

She laughed as he took off at a run, his hand moving to her wrist to make sure she kept up.

Later, he built a fire in the fireplace in his living room.

The orange-yellow flames danced along the top log. "Isn't it a little too hot for that?"

"Not if we're naked," he drawled.

Inside a minute, they stretched with their feet

pointing toward the fire as they lay on the nubby, eggplant-colored rug. "You really ought to invest in a couple of fur throws," she said, wriggling her back on the carpet. "Something with cushion."

"Your ass still sore?"

"What do you think?" Just the mention of that tender body part made it sting.

"Turn over, and I'll give it a rub."

She smiled at the ceiling. "Then my nipples'll get itchy."

"That a bad thing?"

"Guess not," she said breathlessly, as he rolled her then knelt over her thighs, his large, rough palms rubbing her cheeks. The friction warmed her skin.

"I left some marks."

"You don't sound sorry."

"I'm not." His fingers spread. "I can tell where I've been."

"I have another spot that aches," she said, then bit her lip because his hands massaged her ass, and the sensation felt blissful, despite the twinges.

He nudged apart her legs and settled between them. A finger traced her slit. "This the spot?"

"No," she whispered, her pulse racing.

"Lift up, so I can see better," he said in a growly voice.

She groaned but got her knees beneath her to raise her bottom. "You sure do know what to say to a girl to make her feel comfortable."

"Am I supposed to be making you comfortable?"

When his fingers tugged her labia, she giggled and hid her face in her cupped hands.

"This the spot?" he asked, his voice deepening as he trailed a fingertip through her dampening folds and touched her clit.

"That's one of them," she blurted.

Fingers dipped inside her and swirled. "Am I closer?"

"Yes!"

"Thought so." Then his warm breath gusted against her, and his tongue tickled her clit while his fingers thrust deeper and twisted.

She settled her elbows on the carpet and sagged her middle to let the nubby texture abrade her nipples, while he stroked and teased until she was breathing hard and frustrated.

His fingers withdrew, and he planted a kiss against her sex. "We can't fuck here."

"Why not?" Her words came out a bit sharp, because she didn't want him stopping now.

"Rug burn. I don't want to add any new marks."

She pushed up, knelt, then glanced around the room. "The couch, then?"

"Don't want to head to bed?"

"Too far."

He chuckled and rose, reaching down to help her to her feet. She didn't wait for him to guide her into place. Instead, she walked to the sofa and bent over an arm.

"Not where I thought this was going, but *hell yeah*." His hands gripped her ass and parted her. His cock nudged her folds.

Carly quickly realized she wasn't quite tall enough to manage this position. She went to her tiptoes, straining higher as he pushed inside, then groaned when the angle still wasn't right.

"Stop," he said. "I'll go lower."

From the side of her eye, she watched as he shuffled his stance several inches wider. Then he reached past her to plant a hand in the cushion beside her head and pumped. His body jerked against hers.

"You're laughing at me."

He continued stroking inside. "You seriously couldn't wait until we got upstairs?"

"You built a fucking fire. Why waste it?" she gritted out, wishing she could widen her own stance and fit a hand beneath her body to rub her clit.

"And you couldn't just lie lengthwise on the sofa?"

Her body moved with the thrust, but her arousal didn't spike. "I was worried you'd roll off. You're a big guy."

"How big, baby?" he rasped sexily.

"You know damn well you're hung like a donkey."

His laughter filled the room.

Carly couldn't help grinning. His somber mood on the mountain was gone—she'd done that. So, he was laughing at her expense, but she didn't mind so much. She just wished she could get off this way...

"Not getting it?" he drawled.

"I feel like I'm upside down. The blood's rushing to my head."

He pulled free, walked around her then patted the sofa cushion. "Sit here."

"Not a dog," she grumbled, but she pushed back her hair and straightened. She stepped beside him, taking in his scent. Because he didn't move back, she had to crawl onto the cushion and shifted to lie sideways on the couch.

"Uh-huh. Face me."

She turned and sat, lifting a leg to clear his big frame. His cock was at eye level. Moisture filled her mouth as she stared. Hard not to. She'd never seen anything quite so...majestic.

"Not what I was after—I swear," he said, his voice grinding, "but you won't hear any complaints..."

When she glanced up, she found him watching her, the icy blue of his eyes nearly consumed by black pupils. The skin cloaking his cheekbones stretched taut. *Whoever said the way to a man's heart is through his stomach was an idiot.* At that moment, she didn't regret never learning to cook anything other than grilled cheese sandwiches.

Her gaze dropped again to the long, thick cock pulsing every now and then in front of her face. Blinking, she realized that pleasuring Reaper presented a daunting task.

"I don't expect you to deep-throat me or anything," he said quietly. "Don't know if I could explain to the authorities how you choked to death."

Not believing he'd just cracked a joke, her jaw sagged just a little. Then she couldn't help it, she giggled like a teenager, her nose wrinkling, her eyes squinting. Not a pretty sight, she was sure. His lopsided grin made her feel better.

"Whatever you want to do. It'll be great."

If she could get her lips to purse, she might give it a go, but she couldn't stop laughing.

His head fell back, and his hands fisted on his hips.

"Sorry." She giggled again, this time falling sideways on the cushion.

His laughter joined hers—and he grinned so wide she noticed for the first time what perfectly straight white teeth he had. "You have a nice smile."

"Apparently, I also have a formidable dick."

"Yeah, about that." She pushed herself upright and drew a deep breath. Time to prove herself equal to the challenge.

In her experience, which wasn't vast, guys were grateful for any attention paid their manly parts. Although some did get a little impatient when she didn't do it right and had to demonstrate how they liked to be touched. "Tell me if I do this wrong..." Maybe she'd made him wait too long.

He reached down, cupped her hands inside his, and brought them to his shaft. "Wrap them tight, baby. I won't break."

As she tightened her fingers around him, his hands fell away. But she didn't move hers, because she didn't want to irritate the satiny skin that surrounded the hot steel shaft. He needed moisture. And would probably like it from her mouth. *Right, she'd start there.*

Leaning toward him, she stuck out her tongue and

stroked him from the base of his cock up the long side, her tongue drying out before she got to the tip. *Baby steps?* She bent lower and palmed his balls. She liked their weighty feel and the velvety texture of his sac. "You shave."

"I'm polite."

She shot him a frown. "Afraid your girlfriends will have to floss?"

His head canted, and his eyes widened, glaring.

Leaning closer to his balls, she licked the soft velvet surrounding the stones. Not only did she like the texture, she liked the taste and his scent. Musky, but clean. Manly. Her own sex clenched as she sucked a ball into her mouth and licked it all over, moving her lips to tug gently around the sphere.

"*Jesus, fuck.*" His feet shuffled farther apart.

Which forced her lower, but his response gave her encouragement. She sucked the other inside and stroked them both with her tongue. When she drew back, she gripped his cock with renewed determination and dragged it down to point at her mouth.

His hands left his hips and tangled in her hair, but he didn't tug her close. He simply waited as she opened her mouth wide and sucked the tip inside. Her tongue swabbed around and around the head, dipped into the eyelet slit, and then around and around again. When his fingers dug into her scalp, she judged she'd done something right.

Emboldened, she bobbed forward, taking him deeper,

loving the way his girth stretched her mouth, how his soft blunt head caressed her tongue as it traveled back.

When the tip touched the back of her throat, she glanced down his shaft, her eyes crossing.

His chuckle sounded ragged. "Far as you can go, right?"

She swallowed, which had him digging his nails harder into his scalp.

"Damn," he whispered.

So she did it again, and then pulled back, slicked her hands with spit, then gripped him at the base with both hands and took him in her mouth again, this time bobbing forward to meet her fingers, covering every inch of his cock in slick heat. The air around them warmed, and she couldn't tell if the source was the crackling fire or their sexy connection.

Carly wasn't sure how long she moved forward and back, but soon he stroked toward her. She let him, holding still as he fucked her mouth, careful never to push hard against the back of her throat, but seeming to find real pleasure in the way she twisted her hands around his base and sucked with her mouth.

Abruptly, he shoved her backward and bent toward her. He pulled her arm, forcing her to her feet, then pressed his shoulder against her belly. She fell over his shoulder and let out an "eep," as he straightened and headed toward the stairs. "Don't you dare drop me!"

"Won't. Shut up."

Bemused by his brusque tone, she watched the tops

of his buttocks flex as he moved and reached downward to cup them.

"What are you doing?"

"Touching what I'm lookin' at. Got a problem?"

A smack landed on her bottom.

"What was that for?"

"Making sure you're as hot and bothered as I am, sweetheart. This is gonna be quick."

True to his word, a second after he tossed her onto the mattress, he was on top, his very red and swollen cock thrusting through her channel.

As he filled her, she gulped air and raked his back with her nails.

He hooked her knees to raise them and pushed them toward her chest, bending her like a contortionist as he *fucked*. The verb. A powerful, harsh verb which best described the motions as he stroked and stroked, his face getting redder, his gaze more heated.

She cupped his cheeks and lifted her head, the angle of her body making it impossible to breathe, but air was overrated.

His lips were moist, his tongue savage as it thrust inside.

Suddenly, he halted. "Fucking hell," he eased backward.

"No!" She grabbed his shoulders.

"Baby, I forgot. I don't have a condom."

Tingles ran along her skin, and she didn't want to stop the sensation. "It's okay. I'm safe. I'm on the pill."

He gave a savage shake of his head. "I can't promise I am. Gimme a second."

Her breath shuddered out as she considered what he said. She lowered her legs and lay panting on the bed while he rustled inside the drawer of his nightstand. He found what he needed, ripped it open with his teeth, and then hissed as he rolled it down his cock.

"That hurt?"

"No, trying not to blow."

When he lowered himself over her again, he glanced into her face. "Are you okay with this? I can stop. I know I fucked up the moment."

Carly reached up and curved her fingers around the back of his head and pulled his thick hair—hard. "Just finish it."

In the middle of the night, she made him a stack of grilled cheese sandwiches and two more for herself, watching bemused as he consumed them in large, efficient bites. She wore one of his navy T-shirts with the gold Montana Bounty Hunters logo. The shirt fell nearly to her knees. He wore a pair of faded jeans, the top button undone. All that broad, manly chest was bare for her to ogle, which she did, completely unashamed.

When he finished the last one, he met her stare, frowning. "I'll hit the clinic on Monday. Get checked."

She met his frown with one of her own. "Do that."

"You pissed?"

Sighing, she shook her head. "I didn't think you were

a choir boy, but hearing the words was...jolting." She dropped her glance to her coffee cup and circled the rim with a finger. "I know you've probably had hundreds of women."

A scoff sounded. "Not hundreds."

"Dozens," she bit out.

He grimaced then shrugged.

She arched a brow. This conversation was going from bad to worse. "You don't know?"

Brows furrowed, he reached out and placed his hand over hers. "Like you said. I'm not a choir boy."

So, she was just another notch on his bedpost. Her shoulders slumped, and she toyed with the leftover crust of her sandwich.

He cleared his throat. "I've never wanted to be monogamous. Didn't think I could do it."

The way he said it, or maybe the way he stared, with his cool, unblinking gaze, caught her attention. "Is that something...that might change?"

"Let's see..."

Don't push, he meant. But a flicker of hope ignited inside her, and she relaxed. No, she didn't expect this would last forever, but she did hope it would last longer than the term of her ride-along.

He pointed at his empty plate. "Those were good."

With a one-sided smile, she said, "I have a confession."

His eyelids dipped as he stared at her mouth. "You spit in my sandwiches?"

Jerking back her head, she wrinkled her nose. "Who'd

have the guts to do that to you? No, you've tasted the only thing I can cook. Can't even boil eggs—the shells split and the centers turn green."

He chuckled. "I can cook. We won't starve."

"Yeah?" She lifted her coffee cup and peered over the rim. "Who taught you?" Her own mother had a live-in housekeeper who took care of nasty things like cooking and cleaning.

"Learned from an Italian who lived in my barracks when I was in the Marines. Most meals, we had to eat in the mess hall. But on weekends, when we were free, we'd gather money from anyone who wanted a home-cooked meal and buy supplies. He showed me how to make a lot of things."

"So you can make spaghetti?"

He rolled his eyes. "Spaghetti's only the noodles. I make a variety of sauces—bolognaise, marinara, alfredo... I also make lasagna and homemade pizza."

"Hope I'm here long enough for you to cook for me." As soon as she said it, she wished she could take back the statement, because his easy, open expression changed to something a lot less readable. She stood and gathered their dishes. "I'll put these in the dishwasher. I already emptied it." For a few minutes, she kept busy, rinsing and stacking dishes, with her back turned to him, because she didn't want him to know that her eyes were beginning to fill.

The thought of this ending wasn't something she wanted to face. Not yet. She'd been living in the moment, but now she'd placed an expiration date on this...happiness filling her chest.

A chair scraped the floor. His footsteps approached.

When his arms encircled her from behind, she froze for a second, before melting against his chest.

He placed a kiss on her cheek. "Guess you'll have to stay long enough to taste everything I've got," he whispered in her ear.

CHAPTER 7

THE PHONE RANG just before dawn.

Reaper disentangled his arms from around Carly's warm body and reached for his cell. "Yeah, Brian. Do you know what fucking time it is?" he muttered, wiping a hand over his face.

"Sorry to interrupt your beauty sleep, but Fetch has a special job."

Reaper yawned loudly and sat on the edge of the mattress, knowing a "special job" and the time of the call meant sleep was done. "Okay, what's up?"

"Your Class C license still current?"

Reaper frowned in the darkness. "Yeah, what does he need?"

"A semi appears to have been abandoned down the road in Poison at a self-storage business. A military transport. The job's seventy-five thousand if the cargo's still in the back. Ten, if it's not."

Holy crap. Reaper whistled. He glanced at his digital

clock. "I can be there by six AM. Do they know how long it's been sitting?"

"Their dispatch only just started paying attention to the vehicle's GPS tracker when the load didn't make it to the guard headquarters in Helena."

"That's a helluva a detour. Too far to be any accident."

"Yeah, they're pretty sure it's a heist. The rig's been parked about an hour. It's probably already empty. I'll send you the coordinates."

"I'll be on the road in five." He ended the call then glanced at Carly, who was stretching on the bed beside him. "You hear?"

"We leave in five," she said, a yawn stretching her words. "You can give me the details once we're on the road."

Reaper bent and pulled a lock of her hair. "You can stay. Get some sleep." Although, she matched him for stamina, he'd been pretty rough on her body. Neither had gotten much shut-eye, because they'd been so busy gettin' busy.

Her eyebrows rose. "Think I'm gonna miss seeing you drive a big rig?" She shot up off the bed and padded to her open suitcase, sitting beside his dresser. "I'll be inside the Expedition in four." She already pulled out jeans and a long-sleeve tee.

His girl had game. Grinning, Reaper headed to the bathroom.

Once they were on the road, he checked the time and mashed the gas pedal.

She reached for the handle above the passenger-side window. "You're gonna get a ticket."

"Cops around here know I wouldn't speed unless I'm on the job. My driving make you nervous?"

She released the handle. "No. Reflex, I guess. I don't trust many people's driving, but I do yours."

He filled her in on what he knew from Brian's phone call. On a straight stretch of road, he unclipped and handed her his cell. "I can get us to Poison, but once we're there, I'll need you to give me directions. I input the GPS coordinates."

"Is this semi-truck recovery something you do often?" she asked.

Reaper shook his head. "Not much call for it this far from any major city, but my license has come in handy a time or two. Recoveries don't usually pay this well. Mostly, I'm looking for trucks where the driver abandons it, because he's busy getting drunk. One time, I found a rig on the side of the road, completely stripped—all the way down to the wheels. Had to call a big tow truck to haul it back to the owner."

"It's an interesting life you lead, Reaper Stenberg." She shook her head.

"You learning enough to write that book?"

She turned toward him. "I've got enough good stuff for a whole damn series."

He didn't know whether to laugh or cringe. "I thought writers pounded away on typewriters. I haven't even seen you crack open a laptop."

"Laptop's in the bottom of my suitcase." She patted

the knapsack at her feet. "I have an iPad in here I could use, but I'm not ready to write. I'm still doing research. I like to immerse myself in my world to get to know it and my characters first. Everything else, my plot and the developing stakes, just kind of falls into place as I write."

He gave an exaggerated shudder. "Texting even drives me nuts. A hundred-forty characters can frustrate me. I can't imagine writing a book."

"I didn't know I could, but when I left the Army, I had these stories swirling in my head. One morning, I got tired of filling out job applications and opened a Word document. By that evening, I had a complete short story. After that, I was hooked. Of course, that first story was complete shit."

"I don't read much, other than serial killer and real crime books every now and then."

She laughed. "Should I be worried?"

After checking the mirrors for trailing traffic, he chuckled. "Not unless you're a killer. I can spot the psychological traits a mile away."

"Well, my feelings won't be hurt if you never read one of my stories." She grimaced. "Might be better if you never read my bounty hunters books. It could get embarrassing."

He rather liked conversing with her and watching her expressions by the dashboard lights. "So long as the heroine isn't laughing while she's giving a blowjob..."

Her eyebrows lowered. "I already said, I don't write porn."

He shot her a glance, his eyebrows waggling.

"Romance books can get kind of racy..."

"And how would you know?"

"I had a girlfriend who used to read me passages in bed. Things she wanted to try."

Carly giggled. "Is that how you got to be so damn good?"

At the sound of her breathy voice, he cleared his throat. "Maybe we should change the subject, seeing as we don't have time to pull over."

"Okay...how did you get a Class C license?" She grabbed her notebook from her bag and set it on her lap. "Were you a truck driver before you became a badass bounty hunter?"

The way she said "badass bounty hunter" didn't relieve the pressure in his groin...not by a heartbeat. Although, he was pretty sure she could read a passage from the Bible and still make him hot. "I got my training in the Marine Corps. Just another specialization. Mostly, I was just a grunt with a gun."

"You see any action?"

The back of his neck tensed, and he drew a deep breath. "Enough."

"Don't want to talk about it?" she asked, her voice softening.

"I did two tours in Afghanistan. Mostly in the mountains, hunting Al Qaeda." Her nod said she understood what that meant.

"So, the license..."

Glad she didn't want to hear more about his time in the sandbox, he grunted. She seemed to like that sound, because it always made her mouth twitch. "When I got out, I needed a job. I had the experience, and all I needed was the piece of paper. I tested. Only spent six months on the road before I decided the life wasn't for me. I was bored silly." When she yawned, he shot her a quick glance. "Hey, why don't you get more sleep? We'll be there in about forty."

"Sure you don't need company to stay awake? You didn't get any more sleep than I did."

"I'm used to short nights. My jacket's behind you." He lifted an elbow to point. "You can roll it up for a pillow."

With reluctance showing in her frown, she reached behind the seats for his quilted flannel jacket. She brought it to her nose. "Mmm. Smells like you."

He knew exactly what she meant. Just the smell of her shampoo warmed him inside.

"I'll just close my eyes for a few." The seat angled back several inches.

"Go to sleep, Carly."

A minute later, she snored.

After another minute of whining tires and air whooshing from the vents, he realized the drive wasn't near as much fun without her chattering beside him. With her endless curiosity, she kept him on his toes, following the constant segues their conversations took.

Yeah, he liked riding with her at his side. Hell, he liked Carly Wyatt. He would have liked having her for a friend, if they hadn't slept together. But *that* had been inevitable. After one look at her lush figure and pretty face, any intentions he'd had of keeping her at arm's length for the week had been sunk.

The fact she'd been the one to initiate sex still made him smile. The woman charged after what she wanted. He was just happy she wanted him.

He rather liked waking up with her in his bed. Funny, because he'd never before brought a woman to his home. He'd always bedded down at their places. Less chance of the ladies leaving things behind that required them staying past their expiration to pack their shit. He wasn't proud that he felt that way. That he'd never felt a connection deep enough he regretted being booted out the door.

But Carly was different—smarter, and fierce in her own way. A lot like his partner, Jamie. He thought the two women would get along like gangbusters if they ever met. That thought got him considering how he might make that happen. He wondered if Carly might agree to be his "plus one" for the wedding, then blinked and let out a slow breath. The possibility didn't make him itch...

Reaper turned on the radio and kept the volume low, listening to a news channel—anything rather than continuing with plans for a future Carly probably didn't want.

He woke her once he passed the Poison, Montana city limits sign.

She brought her seat upright and activated his phone to get directions to the truck. Minutes later, they turned into ABC Storage's parking lot.

Reaper drove slowly, halting at the end of the first row to gaze down the line of storage units, making sure no one else was about. They found the truck behind the second row, tucked in beside the garbage bins. The back of the rig faced them, a heavy-duty padlock still securing the shackle. *Whoa, did we just hit the jackpot?*

"The lock's still there. That's a good sign, right?" Carly sat forward in her seat.

"You stay put." He let himself out of the SUV and stepped to the rear of his vehicle, opened the back gate, and rooted beneath the various tools he kept for a bolt cutter.

Carly joined him as he strode to the back of the big rig.

"Thought I said—"

"I heard you. But I want to see what's inside, too."

He handed her the tool. "I'm checking the cab first, to make sure the driver's not there sleeping off a hangover." Although, he didn't really think the driver had gotten disoriented and wound up in this podunk town by accident. He pulled his Glock from his holster, ignoring Carly's widening eyes.

Standing at the rear of the rig, he glanced over his shoulder. "Keep a lookout," he whispered. "You see anyone approach, you jump in my truck and book it."

She shook her head. "I won't leave you."

"I can take care of myself." As he moved down the side of the gray trailer, he kept his weapon in front of him and breathed slow. He was pretty sure the driver was long gone, but he'd learned not to take any situation for granted. Thieves were stupid, but they could also be deadly.

At the door, he reached up and quietly flipped the door handle, listening intently for any noises inside the vehicle, but he heard nothing. He stepped up to dart a glance inside the cab. The space was empty, so he climbed inside and searched behind the seats, looking for anything that might explain why the driver had dumped his rig. Other than trash from half-eaten meals, he found nothing. The keys were tucked atop the sun visor.

He climbed down and headed back to Carly. "I've got keys. Let's see what he was hauling." Using the bolt cutters, he cut the lock. When he opened the back gate, his chest expanded. The trailer was packed floor-to-ceiling with plastic-wrapped cargo cartons marked laptops. "Holy fuck. Babe, we've got to get out of here quick. Whoever's behind this job isn't giving up a haul like this without a fight. Has to be worth more than a million." He closed the gate and secured it with another lock he'd carried in his pocket. "Come with me."

Back at his Expedition, he pulled out a pair of walkie-talkie radios. "Here, the in-ear devices'll be useless on the road. They don't have the range." He clipped a small radio to her belt beside her hip, and then slid the wire over her ear for the earpiece he tucked into her ear. He attached the mic button to the collar of her tee, dropped the cord inside her shirt, and plugged it into the radio. "If you keep close enough, we won't have to use our phones." He donned his own radio and earpiece and turned it on. Then he pressed the mic button. "You hear me?"

She nodded and smiled. "Loud and clear."

"Only one of us can talk at a time. So pause whenever you want me to say something back."

"Will do. I promise I'll stay close, and I won't leave a scratch on your paint." She bounced on her toes. "This is exciting—we're stealing a rig from a gang of crooks!"

He gave her a narrowed glare. "This recovery job isn't fun, sweetheart. It's damn dangerous."

"Got it."

Her eager expression didn't change a bit. He sighed. "Drive my truck between the storage unit rows and wait for me to back out. Once we're on the road, we're not stopping for anything until we hit Helena." He hoped like hell the semi had the fuel to make good on that promise.

Carly bobbed her head. "My bladder'll last."

A grin tugged at his mouth. "Good to know." He bent and kissed her hard. "Stay safe."

"Babe, I've got this." She gave him a wink.

ONCE THEY WERE AGAIN on the two-lane highway, heading south toward the interstate, Carly's initial excitement morphed into a bad case of nerves. Which only got worse when they turned onto the interstate and met more traffic. Any one of the vehicles they passed could hold the bad guys. All the scenarios of what might happen along the way played in her head. She gripped the steering wheel so hard her knuckles turned white.

Reaper's warning that their situation was "damn dangerous" repeated in her head.

"You're not talking. Anything wrong?" Reaper's voice sounded in her ear.

His drawling tone usually incited her into doing something to make him smile. She didn't feel very funny right now. She pressed her mic button. "I'm here."

A loud exhalation sounded. "You nervous?"

"D'ya think? I'm following a million-dollar cargo down the road that some gang intended to rob." She glanced on the rear view mirror for headlights but saw none. Sunlight was peeking over the horizon.

"I should have called Dag or Jamie. Hell, if you like, turn around. I don't need the company."

"And leave you without backup?"

"Baby, you are *not* my backup. Anything goes sideways, all I'll expect from you is to call the cops and get the hell away."

"Then why did you let me come?" A long silence followed, and she wondered if he'd forgotten to press his button.

"I let you come because I'm selfish. I like your company."

"You do?" She couldn't help the happy lift in her voice.

"Just wish I'd had a clue what was inside the truck."

"How much longer to Helena?"

"Sticking to the speed limit, the drive will be a couple hours."

"And if you don't?"

"You up to flooring it?" he asked, a hint of a smile in his voice.

"Hey, I drove in downtown Denver. I can handle a little speed."

The truck in front of her pulled away. She gunned the engine to keep pace. "Think they're behind us?"

"Don't know which direction they'd come from. But they know which roads we're taking. They know we're heading straight to Helena with the load. Choices are limited because of the size of this vehicle. I'm not too worried so long as we're I-90, but we exit near Garrison to cut across to Helena. Highway 12 is two lanes. It doesn't get much traffic, and it's narrow."

Her heart pounded faster. "So, if they're following us, that's where they'd hit us?"

"Me, babe. Not you. Don't even think about intervening. You find a safe place to pull over. Make a call. That's all I want you to do. Hear me?"

The serious tone in his voice sobered her. She nodded, but realized he couldn't see her agreement. She pressed her button. "Yeah. I call."

"I wouldn't worry too much. We're a long way gone. Once they realize the truck's not where it was stashed, they'll probably scatter."

Her hands started aching, so she eased her hold. Doing so somehow helped the rest of her body relax. "So, after we leave Helena...?"

"I'll have to stop by Kalispell and turn in the paperwork to Fetch. The office's on our way. He'll want to get it completed and filed so we get paid."

Happy to be thinking about the time *after* this job was done, she asked, "What are you doing with your cut?"

"I don't know. I need to rent a bush hog."

"That a bulldozer?"

"Yeah. Something to knock down some brush and take out some stumps. My place needs a yard."

She knew what he was doing—switching to another subject to keep her calm. And she appreciated the effort, knowing he wasn't the most talkative man. "Does it dig holes?"

"Why do you ask?" he drawled.

It was like he knew she was going to tease him. "Because you need a koi pond in your front yard, don't you think?" Her lips spread into a wide smile in anticipation of his answer.

After he'd stopped chortling about goldfish icicles, she felt better. "Reaper?"

"Yeah, baby?"

"I like when you call me that."

A few seconds passed in silence.

The worry she might have crossed into "needy-clingy" land again rose.

But then he cleared his throat. "If I dig a hole, will you figure out how we keep it hot enough in a Montana winter?"

He's said "we" and "winter." And he'd had enough time to think through what he was going to say, which meant that the words were deliberate. Dear God, she was falling in love with the man.

CHAPTER 8

Ten minutes after they turned off I-90 onto the two-lane highway leading straight to Helena, Reaper's cellphone buzzed.

Holding the phone next to the steering wheel, he ran his thumb up the screen and saw he had a text from Sammy. Frowning, he pressed the message.

Sammy: You on the road, bro?

Reaper hit voice. "Yeah. Not in Bear Lodge. You need something?"

Sammy: Who's in the rig?

Reaper's stomach dropped. "Me. My girl's in my vehicle. What the fuck's going on?

Sammy: I'll take care of her. Ditch the truck. You got trouble ahead.

In his side mirror, he watched as a truck passed his SUV then abruptly slowed.

The SUV ran off the shoulder into the ditch.

Fuck! Tossing away the phone, he hit his mic button. "Baby, we're about to be hit. You run into the woods!"

He lifted his foot off the gas as the rig entered a bend in the highway, hoping he'd spot a place to pull over. Ahead, two vehicles sat parked sideways in the road, blocking both lanes. The shoulder wasn't wide enough for him to get around, so he slammed on the brakes, stopping mere feet away from the vehicles.

Staring through the windshield, he watched as Blacky McNally stepped from behind one of the trucks and raised a rifle. Holding up his left hand, hoping to stall for time, Reaper unclipped his seatbelt with the other, then dove sideways in his seat. A shot rang out, and glass sprinkled down. When he twisted, he saw a hole in the headrest.

His chest tightened. Blacky didn't intend to let him live.

With Reaper's urgent voice still ringing in her ears, Carly grabbed her cellphone from the dash, slammed open her door, and leapt to the ground. In the distance, she heard a loud whine and the screech of tires, and knew Reaper fought to stop the truck. Hoping like hell he made it to the safety of the woods, she didn't have time to say a prayer. She had her own problems. The pickup that cut her off was stopped. She ran around the back of Reaper's SUV then darted across the ditch and straight into the woods.

"Lady, stop!"

Like hell. With no idea what was happening now that Reaper was out of sight, her first priority, the one thing she absolutely could not fail to do, was follow the plan. With her heart racing wildly, she reached the trees and slid behind a tall fir. She hit Brian's number on speed dial and glanced back toward the road.

A tall figure ran in her direction.

A cold shiver hitting her spine, she pulled her Berretta from her holster.

"Carly?" Brian's voice sounded in her ear.

"We've got trouble," she whispered as loudly as she dared. "On Highway 12, maybe ten miles from I-90. We're being hit."

"I'll call the Montana Highway Patrol. Get somewhere safe."

She ended the call and stuffed her phone in the back pocket of her jeans. With her Berretta held close to her chest, she took a deep breath and darted a glance between the trees.

The man approaching her held up both hands. "Lady, it's Sammy. Reaper's brother. I won't hurt you."

His brother? She remembered what Reaper had said about his brother hanging around with the wrong people. "Don't come any closer. I have a gun." *And I don't want to kill Reaper's brother, even if he is a criminal.*

"Ma'am, swear I don't mean you any harm," he said, his words coming fast. "But we don't have time for this shit. We have to help my brother. They're gonna kill him."

Another chill shivered down her spine, and she knew

that if what he said was true, she had to take the risk. Remembering the way Reaper had spoken about his brother, she knew he would never give up on Sammy. And sincerity filled Sammy's words. She lowered her weapon and stepped out from behind the tree. "Reaper carries weapons in the back of the Expedition."

With a nod, he turned and sped back toward the highway.

In a few strides she made up the distance and followed on his heels. At the vehicle, she opened the back gate.

Sammy pushed her aside and rifled through Reaper's gear bag, pulling out what looked like flash-bang grenades, stuffing them into the large pockets of his black cargo pants, and then picking up a rifle. "You stay here." He shut the gate and headed toward the front of the SUV.

Gunfire sounded in the distance. She ran for the passenger side door and climbed inside as he started the engine.

"I can see why he likes you," Sammy muttered, pulling back onto the road and hitting the gas. "You don't listen worth shit."

Just around the bend, Carly saw the rig, the cab doors still shut, two vehicles parked sideways in the middle of the highway in front of the semi. More gunfire sounded, rapid-fire, and she saw figures dart up from behind one of the vehicles to fire toward the semi. She couldn't see Reaper, but she heard single shots, likely from Reaper's handgun.

He's still alive. Adrenaline must have been flying through her veins, because time slowed, and she felt a fierce resolve to save him strengthen her muscles.

"Get on the floor," Sammy shouted and turned the wheel to head around the truck, not slowing.

She ducked down to the floorboard and gasped when shots sounded and glass shattered above her, glittering fragments raining down on the seat she'd occupied.

Barely breathing, she glanced toward Sammy. His face was screwed up in a frightening grimace as he gripped the wheel. Another spray of bullets pinged against the vehicle. Sammy ducked and hit the brakes. "Brace yourself!"

The crash rocketed her headfirst into her seat. The driver's side air bag popped and shot back to slam against Sammy. When she bounced back to the floor, she saw Sammy swiping at the quickly deflating white bag and gripping his shoulder. Then he reached into his pockets and tossed her the grenades, opened his door, and slid out, rifle in hand.

She leaned toward her door, looked up to see the cab of the big rig, just in time to spot a hand raise and point a weapon toward the trucks ahead. Reaper was firing blindly, maybe giving them cover.

Hoping the men in the trucks weren't looking her way, she pushed open her door and dropped to the ground, crouching behind the steel door as she pulled a pin then lobbed the first grenade behind one of the trucks. An explosion sounded. Smoke rose. Without waiting to see the men's reactions, she pulled the pin on a second grenade and tossed it behind the second truck.

Then she raised her Berretta and aimed over the space between the door and the SUV, as men shouted and scrambled away from behind the trucks. She drew a slow, steady breath, held it, and pulled the trigger. Her shot struck one of the thieves in the side.

A shot sounded from the other side of her vehicle, and she glanced across to see Sammy with the rifle balanced on the window frame as he fired.

In the distance, the high-pitched whine of sirens sounded. But she kept her gaze ahead, pulling on her training—training she'd never had to use in a live-fire situation during her deployment in the desert. She fired again and again, but her Berretta clicked. Out of bullets. So she ducked inside the SUV for another grenade.

And suddenly, the firing stopped.

She peeked through the windshield. One of the trucks was pulling away, bodies diving for the truck bed. The truck picked up speed for a couple hundred feet, but then brake lights flashed.

Police cruisers with flashing lights approached. The truck made a screaming U-turn, but now faced the SUV. Sammy raised his rifle and shot into the air. A clear warning they weren't getting past him.

Then sirens sounded behind Carly, and she whipped around her head.

Deputies slammed open doors and hunkered behind them, weapons raised.

A voice, amplified by a bullhorn, stated, "Drop your weapons and move away from your vehicles."

Breathing out her relief, she dropped the grenade into the seat and held up her hands, then turned to look toward the semi.

Reaper climbed out and dropped straight to the ground, not glancing once toward the police cruisers. In two long strides, he enfolded her inside his arms, lifting her from the ground. His hand gripped the back of her hair. "You don't listen for shit, woman."

Amazingly his gruff, complaining voice calmed her. Carly closed her eyes, hearing the deputies on their loudspeakers, but she figured they wouldn't fire at a couple hugging. To hell with them. To hell with everyone. Needing what this big man offered, she wrapped herself around him and held on tight.

CARLY SAT with her legs hanging over the edge of the back gate of the Expedition, drinking a cup of hot coffee one of the deputies poured from a thermos. He'd seen her shaking and must have thought she was cold. The coffee did help warm her, and her jaw was finally relaxing enough she could take sips. Feeling like a weenie, she admitted to herself and the cute deputy, she'd never been so scared in her entire life.

The aftermath was all rather surreal. After the pair had been forced to their knees by law enforcement, deputies swarmed the highway, divesting all the combatants of their weapons. Reaper flashed his bounty hunter's badge, and then had to explain her role before they'd been allowed to stand.

"So, do all writers assist in shootouts for the sake of research?" the cute deputy drawled.

Carly snorted and took another sip, happy to be alive. Happy Reaper had made it. Two of the gang hadn't been so lucky. The one she'd hit was being loaded into an ambulance. She was relieved she hadn't killed him and took no satisfaction from the news the EMT provided. "That boy's going to be shitting in a bag for the rest of his life."

No, she was glad her life didn't usually require she make life-and-death choices. She'd just as soon store her Berretta in a box and never wrap her fingers around the grip again.

"Feds are here." The deputy tipped his hat before striding away.

The next hour stretched. She figured the exhaustion gnawing at her body was the result of the letdown of adrenaline. From her seat, she watched as FBI agents and forensics techs scoured the scene. The gang members still on their feet were loaded into a panel truck and driven away.

Sammy leaned against a police cruiser, his arm in a sling due to his dislocated shoulder, giving his statement to an agent. Reaper stood next to him, his expression set.

While anyone else looking at him might have thought he had it together, she read the worry in his eyes. After they'd been allowed to move freely, he'd patted down her body to make sure she was okay and given her a hard kiss.

Then he'd set her on the open back of his vehicle and wagged a finger in front of her face. "Do not move from this spot." After that, he'd been with Sammy.

An action she understood, because he'd be worried about his brother's disposition. The fact that he'd turned on his friends at the last minute to save their lives was a good thing. So was the fact he was giving up everything he knew about the gang's criminal activities. Still, he'd be serving some hard time. And jail wouldn't be a safe place for him, not when he'd informed on his club.

She looked up to see a set of familiar figures and smiled at their approach.

Brian Cobb's wheelchair looked incongruous as he sped past the multiple law enforcement vehicles lined up along the road. Fetch's burly frame, salt-n-pepper hair and beard, and piercing slate gaze were a comforting sight. She didn't ask how they'd made it past the Feds. Fetch must have pull in high places.

Brian rolled up to a stop in front of her. His narrowed gaze searched them before he spoke. "Glad to see you two made it." A grin stretched across his thin face. "Heard you were *badass*."

She held up a trembling hand. "Not so bad, but at least my ass is still intact."

Fetch chuckled and moved closer to give her a bear hug. "How's my favorite writer?"

"You did warn me things would be hopping if I rode with Reaper..."

Leaning back, he gave her sharp-eyed look. "We can give you a lift back."

She cut a glance toward Reaper, who was looking right at her.

His right eye dipped in a slow wink then he turned back to the investigator interviewing Sammy.

"I think I'll hang here for a while." She gave Fetch a little smile.

One dark eyebrow rose. "That *thing* we talked about it. You give it any thought?"

"I'll let you know," she said, feeling a flush rise in her cheeks. Fetch was far too observant, and had likely figured out something was going on between her and Reaper. *Did the man have to wink? In front of his boss, even.*

"I'm checking with the Feds," Fetch said. "They're talking about holding up that truck for their forensics folks to comb over the cab. I'm working on securing the release of the trailer itself. I have another driver coming with a rig to haul it." He gave her a little salute then walked away.

Brian gripped his wheels, preparing to go. "Don't know what all of that was about, but if it has anything to do with you sticking around..." He gave her a grin. "I don't think Reaper would complain too much either."

"Brian..." Putting her hands on her hip, she glared. "You won't be the first to know."

"Of course. Guess I better head back to the van. See you guys."

Grateful the men had checked in, she gave him a wave then sat staring into her cup. The coffee had gone cold. Tipping the cup, she emptied the contents on the ground. Two large feet entered her view, and she glanced up to find Reaper standing over her. She shot a glance toward Sammy and saw him being helped into the back of an unmarked black car. "Is he okay?" she asked quietly.

"He'll need a good lawyer, but they've promised not to put him in general population. Depending on what he can give them so far as the club's criminal activities go, he may be offered a deal."

"That's good, right?" she asked, looking into his face and noting the creases around his mouth were deeper.

Reaper's smile was a little sad. "I told him we'll keep in better touch. That I'll visit. I'll help him anyway I can, including making sure he has the best attorney money can buy. Which means, I'll be taking on as many of the high-fee bounty jobs I can."

"Fetch is working to get the FBI to shake that rig free."

"Yeah, but I won't be behind the wheel." His gaze locked with hers. "I'm taking you home."

Worried he was losing out on money he'd need, she shook her head. "I can catch a ride—Brian can't have gotten far—"

He pressed a straight finger against her mouth. "No," he said, leaning closer. "Dag's on his way. They're keeping my vehicle. We'll have to clear it if you want to keep your bag."

"I'm sorry about your Expedition. It's going to need some work."

Shaking his head, he grunted. "My insurance is

already through the roof. It's not your fault. Come on." He held out his hand.

Once hers was firmly in his grasp, she let him lead her away, sighing inside, because she wasn't sure about his mood.

Dag dropped them at the cabin then snapped a little salute as he backed down the driveway.

Reaper unlocked the front door and held it for Carly as she crossed his threshold. She'd been quiet on the drive back, for the most part. Chatting with Dag about inconsequential shit, like movies they'd watched and places they'd traveled. Nothing to do with the job. Not a single word about today's fiasco.

She'd barely glanced at him, sitting in the back. Maybe because he'd rested his head against the headrest and angled his gaze to watch the forest blur past his window. Ever since he'd watched his brother get handcuffed and led away, he'd felt numb. Again, he'd failed him. Sammy was bound for jail.

He still couldn't believe Sammy's friends had been tied up in the heist. What dumb fucking luck was that? The second he'd seen Sammy's texts, he'd known, in his gut, that the day wouldn't end well.

They'd all nearly died. The thought of what could have happened to Carly made his stomach sour. He remembered how excited she'd been when they'd found the rig, then how she'd gotten more and more nervous along the journey toward Helena. He'd talked her down, had her laughing, and then everything went to shit.

Thank God, Sammy had been the one to cut her off on the road.

If the pursuer had been anyone else in that gang, she'd be dead. All the way back to his cabin, he couldn't erase the picture out of his mind of her lying on the forest floor with a bullet in her chest.

Then he'd thought about what he would have felt if he'd lived and she hadn't. Every bit of joy would have been sucked out of him. And how could that be? They'd only known each other a few days. Now the thought of her not being alive, of not being somewhere safe and happy, made his chest ache. Was this what loving a woman felt like?

Inside the cabin, she dropped her bag on the sofa then looked back at him.

Her skin was pale, and her left cheek smudged with dirt. Sprinkles of safety glass glittered on her shoulders and in her hair. "You need a shower."

She wrinkled her nose. "Do I smell that bad?"

Shaking his head, he walked closer, lifting a finger to brush off a speck of the glass. "You've got bits of glass all over you. It won't cut you, but you don't want it getting in your eyes."

"So do you." She flicked a speck on his shirt. "Want to help me wash it off?"

That quick, she pulled him in. He let out a deep breath. "You sure you want to—with me? Baby, I almost got you killed," he whispered, his voice getting rough because his throat had tightened.

She gripped his shirt in her fist and pulled him closer. "You blaming yourself? Because I'm a grown-ass woman, and I remember insisting I go along."

"You should have stayed in the trees." He lowered his forehead to rest against hers.

"I couldn't. Not after I heard that first shot." Her eyes filled, but she smiled. "If I'd done nothing, I couldn't have lived with myself."

"Don't cry," he growled and lifted a thumb to her cheek.

She blinked and took a deep breath. "I won't."

But her lower lip trembled, so he did the only thing he could think of doing to make it stop. He tipped up her chin and kissed her.

They swayed closer, bodies pressing together as their hands roamed. He knew what she was experiencing. He had to be sure she wasn't hurt. He skimmed her shoulders, her breasts, her back and down to that nice, round ass. When he pulled back his head, they were both breathing hard and her mouth was open, her breaths coming in short pants. "Shower," he said, turning her with his hands on her shoulders then giving her butt a swift pat.

Slowly, she moved toward the stairs, and then sped up them.

He smiled, watching her run. Then he followed, taking them two at a time.

By the time they reached the shower in the master

bedroom, they were both breathless. They stripped, kicking their clothes into a corner before stepping into the stall.

He washed her hair, standing behind her and tipping back her head to make sure the glass crystals didn't run into her eyes. Then he knelt on one knee as she did the same for him. When they were clean, he rubbed her dry and blotted the water from his body.

Entering the bedroom, he closed the curtains to block out the sun, turned off all the lights, except the one beside the bed. Then he cloaked himself before slipping under the covers and drawing her close.

She curled against his side. "I can't believe it's all been just one day."

"Everything, since the minute we met, has moved at warp speed."

She chuckled. "Are you a Trekkie?"

As he angled his head to look down at her, he smiled. "Used to watch re-runs with my little brother when we were kids. I wanted to be Captain Kirk. He pretended to be Mr. Spock. He was always telling me to 'live long and prosper'. Or giving me Spock's special nerve pinch, and I'd pretend to pass out."

"I'm glad you have that." Her hand rested on his chest. "My sister was older than me. Born old, I think. She never played with me."

Again, he thought it strange that he could be so happy, just talking with her in the dark about silly things. Any other woman and he'd already be inside her, ready to finish and get the hell away. "What sorts of things would you have wanted her to do? Did you like Barbies?"

"I liked He-Man," she said. "And Thundercat. Barbie was always looking for a hero to save her ass."

That comment hit home. He pulled her closer. "You saved mine."

"We saved each other," she whispered. Her kiss landed on his cheek then slid across to his mouth. "Almost missed your face entirely," she said, laughter in her voice.

He pulled her over his body, arranging her position for his satisfaction, folding her thighs beside his hips, while he cupped her breasts and molded them with his palms. "Put me inside you, Carly."

Without fumbling, she found his shaft and centered it, then slowly lowered herself, pulsing downward until he was buried inside. "You shouldn't fit at all," she grumbled, pausing her movements. "Does it squish down at the top? Because I know how long it is."

A grin stretched his mouth. "It doesn't squish. Does it feel like it has an inch of give?"

Her hands cupping the backs of his, she began to rise and fall. "You've probably spoiled sex for dozens of women."

"How's that?" He shook off her hands then gave her nipples a twist and toggled them with a rough fingertip.

"Because no one will else will ever feel the way you do. I can feel every inch of you inside me."

"You must have spoiled your dozen boyfriends, because I can swear I've never felt this way either."

"Really?"

The surprised note in her voice gave him courage. He reached out and pulled her down, and then rolled over her body, never breaking the connection. Next, he bracketed her face between his palms as he moved, keeping his rhythm even, his strokes flowing forward and back. "You've changed my mind about some things," he whispered, leaning downward to caress her mouth with his. "I never wanted to be monogamous. Didn't think I could want just one woman."

She stretched upward and bit his bottom lip. "And now you think you can?"

He nearly groaned at the huskier inflection of her voice. "I can if it's you."

Her chest pushed against his with her deep inhalation. Below, he felt her walls tighten around his cock. He slipped his hands under her bottom, cradling her as he rocked inside her slick heat. "I could stay like this forever."

"Please don't," she said in a little voice. Her fingernails dug into his ass. "Move faster."

He'd do her one better. He pulled free, then hooked his arms beneath her knees and raised her ass off the bed. Holding her in place, he nudged her once and thrust inside.

Carly pulled her lower lip between her teeth and closed her eyes.

"Baby, play with your clit."

Both arms reached, pressing her tits together. She pulled up the top of her folds, exposing the swollen knot and began rubbing it. As her face screwed up into an aroused grimace, Reaper was sure he'd never seen anything sexier. He hammered faster, pulling her hard against him as he stroked forward. Over and over, until she stopped rubbing and crushed the sheets at her sides in her fists.

"Reaper!"

Her scream sent him over the crest. Several more times, he stroked, grunting with the power of his eruption. He slowed his motions, but continued rocking because he didn't want the connection to end—ever.

When at last he let go of her legs and lowered himself over her heaving body, he nuzzled into the corner of her neck. "I fucking love you..."

Her breath hitched then slowly released. "You don't just love fucking me?" she asked, her words coming in a fast whisper. "Or do you...love me?"

He raised his head and framed her face with both hands. "Will you stay, Carly? Here. In this house, with me?"

She shook her head. "I want to go back to what you just said. Do you love me? Because if you do, I—"

Oh crap, he'd blurted it too soon. He kissed her hard, halting her words. When he lifted his head, he glared. "You don't have to say it back. Not if you're not there yet. Just...stay." He held still, feeling his stomach knot as she took her sweet time responding.

"Reaper?"

"Yes, baby."

"Um, how mad would you be if I told you I'm your new partner?"

His emotions pinged between happy and pissed. He swallowed hard, and then his heartbeat pounded at his temple. "You and Fetch work this out before you came?"

"He offered me the job. Said to think about it." Her gaze fell to where her fingers played with the tip of his ponytail. "Said Sky was considering hiring on, and he'd like him to work with Jamie, seeing as they've worked so well together...before..."

"Carly...?"

She peeked from beneath her lashes. "Yes, Reaper?"

"What about your writing?"

"Well, the thing is, I can write anywhere." A bare shoulder shrugged. "Anytime. I can work around—"

He kissed her again. "Are you moving in with me?"

"If you think—" At his glare, she gave a nod. "Yes."

He let out a deep breath. "Guess I'd prefer to have you where I can keep an eye on you."

Her smile was quick. "So, you don't mind?"

"I said I love you." He narrowed his gaze.

"Oh. You're still waiting..." She licked her lower lip. "I think I figured out how I felt when you told me you'd dig a koi pond. Any man who'd do a crazy thing like that—"

"Dammit," he said softly.

"Okay already." She closed her eyes, took a deep breath, and then said, "I love you, too."

When she looked at him again, her pretty whisky-colored eyes were filled with so much yearning his chest tightened. "Was that so hard?"

"Since I've never said that to another living soul—yes."

He slipped his arms beneath her and cradled her against his body. Sure, he had no doubts she'd give him at least one heart attack a week, but he couldn't imagine not riding with her beside him. "You won't put yourself in danger ever again. You'll be smart. Listen to what I say."

"Of course, I will." Her brows wrinkled. "Unless a bride is ready to beat you with a bouquet..."

The mention of a bride didn't make him cringe. Not even one bit.

CHAPTER 9

Isaiah Watson was up on charges for armed robbery. His bail had been set at a $200,000. His mother secured the bond with the deed for the hair salon she'd owned and operated for twenty-five years. She'd called from the courthouse to insist that Montana Bounty Hunters find her son after he'd failed to appear for his trial. She'd even provided the names of his girlfriend, his friends, and the bar he frequented. Because Fetch had been the one to bond him out, she'd still had his card in her wallet. She wanted her asshole son found and didn't care if he got roughed up a bit along the way back to jail.

Isaiah wasn't a smart man. He'd bragged to friends at the Blue Elk Tavern in Libby that he wasn't going to jail. Instead, he would head into the mountains to live off the land, using his skills as a hunter to survive. He didn't need no Walmart or no woman. No, he was going "off the grid."

Well, "off the grid" turned out to be a vacation cabin

on the edge of the Koontenai National Forest he'd broken into and now currently occupied. Reaper guessed the first night Isaiah had slept in a tent on the cold hard ground, he'd probably rethought his future.

"Yeah, he's in there," came Jamie's voice in his ear. "He's in the kitchen cooking something on the stove. Smells like Dinty Moore canned stew."

Reaper's stomach rumbled. They'd been tracking Isaiah for a day and a half from the point where one of his drinking buddies dropped him on the road. Jamie's dog, Tessa, led the team over rugged terrain—down gullies and up high ridges, finding the remains of one cold campfire and protein bar wrappers along the way. Reaper wolfed down the same brand of bar that morning for breakfast and resented the fact Isaiah was helping himself to a hot meal, thanks to the generator that rumbled on the cabin porch.

"Don't suppose we can finish his stew once we have him in cuffs."

Reaper gave his new trainee a sideways glance and shrugged. "Fetch is gonna take a couple of hours to get here with the van. I just sent him the GPS coordinates. Don't see why not."

Carly smiled from her position hunkered down beside the front porch.

"Let's take down this knucklehead," Sky said from his position on the far side of the cabin. "Hope he hasn't emptied the pantry."

Reaper crept quietly onto the porch and tried the

door handle, which twisted under his hand. "Remember, he's armed. And he's sworn not to be taken alive."

"Yeah, and he said he was going to live off the land like Jeremiah Johnson," Jamie muttered. "I don't think he'll give us much of a fight."

Hoping that case would turn out to be true, Reaper took a deep breath. "On three, folks. One, two...three." With his weapon raised, he pushed open the door and entered the living room, heading toward the kitchen tucked into the right side of the cabin. Carly crept right behind him.

A crash sounded from the rear of the cabin, and Reaper almost smiled. Jamie had always insisted on using less destructive ways of getting into domiciles, but he must have rubbed off on her a bit.

Then he heard footsteps, rushing his way from the kitchen, and he ducked to hide beside the kitchen door. Carly took the opposite side.

When Isaiah burst through the opening, she stuck out her foot.

Isaiah jumped over it but didn't miss the arm Reaper shot out to catch him in the gut. Isaiah bounced back and landed on his ass, then scrambled on his hands and knees back into the kitchen, heading straight for the gun leaning against the pantry door.

But Jamie rushed him, jumping on his back, her arm around his neck in a chokehold.

Isaiah reared upward and stood, shaking his shoulders and backing into the counter, scraping her against its length.

Carly pushed past Reaper and hit Isaiah and Jamie with a flying tackle, knocking both to the floor. The trio rolled side to side, grunting and groaning, Isaiah still trying to free himself, but the women held on for dear life.

"Think we should lend a hand?" Sky drawled, stepping through the door with Tessa at his side.

The dog growled and lunged against the lead.

Reaper watched Carly get in a few digs against Isaiah's ribs and nodded.

The two men shared a glance, and then Sky reached down to release the clip on Tessa's leash.

Tessa shot forward, entering the only space on Isaiah's body not covered by determined women. She opened her jaws and clamped down on his crotch.

Isaiah screamed like a little girl—high-pitched and piercing—and stopped moving.

The women moved back and stood, both looking disheveled but grinning.

Jamie dropped to a knee beside Tessa. "Good girl, *aus!*"

Tessa released Isaiah then moved backward, her gaze never leaving the trembling, whimpering man.

Ready to finalize the capture, Reaper slipped his handcuffs from his back pocket and stepped forward, "Isaiah Watson, we're Fugitive Recovery Agents. Roll onto your stomach and put your hands behind your back."

Isaiah eyed the dog, who issued a low rumbling growl, and quickly rolled.

Reaper secured him, and then helped him up and into a chair.

"Anyone gonna look at my balls?" he whined. "Fuckin' dog bit me."

Jamie frowned and bent toward the skinny man. "I don't see any holes in your jeans. She did not bite."

"Well, she crushed 'em." He rocked back and forth in the chair. "You have to get me to a doctor."

Reaper sighed. "Stand up."

Isaiah slid forward then stood. Reaper unbuckled the bail-jumper's belt and shoved down his pants.

The women whipped around, giving the men their backs. "Not something I need to see," muttered Carly.

Reaper grimaced and pushed down the other man's tighty-whities.

Sky and Reaper stared downward.

"Look good to me." Sky pressed his mouth into a straight line.

"You have to look under 'em," Isaiah said. "It's where it hurts."

"I am not picking up your balls," Reaper bit out, giving the man a scowl.

Jamie sputtered, and her shoulders shook. Carly leaned against her side, her entire body quivering.

Sky blew out a breath and rifled through the kitchen drawers. He handed Reaper a spatula.

This task was what he got for being team leader. Reaper blew out a breath between pursed lips, then caught Carly glancing over her shoulders, her eyes dancing with merriment. He gave a little shake of his head, warning her of dire consequences if she laughed aloud.

But that only managed to make her silent laughter shake her body harder.

Reaper tucked the spatula under the man's balls and lifted them. "You have a look, Sky."

Shaking his head, Sky held up his hands. "Hey, I found the tool. It's all on you, now."

Cussing under his breath, Reaper took a knee and peered, not too closely, at the man's balls. "Don't see any injury. I think you'll be fine."

"But they're swollen, man."

Reaper gave him a cold glare. "Ask for an icepack when you get to jail." He tossed away the spatula and pulled up the guy's underwear and pants. "Now, sit."

His teammates applauded.

Jamie and Carly got busy in the kitchen, heating up cans of stew and chili on the stove.

Sky found some rope in a shed and tied Isaiah's feet and one hand, leaving a hand free for him to join their impromptu meal.

As they ate, the women chattered.

"Let me see that rock, again." Carly waited as Jamie held out her hand to show off her engagement ring.

Reaper shot a glance toward Sky and cocked an eyebrow.

Sky leaned close and whispered, "I'll send you the address of the jeweler."

Reaper nodded, waiting for a second to see whether

his balls shriveled or his stomach knotted, but all he felt was a sweet resolve.

Carly caught his stare and gave him a wink.

Was she expecting him to propose? They'd only known each other a month. Yes, they'd been living together for all that time, but still...

He reached for her hand and gave it a squeeze, not blushing when Sky and Jamie shared knowing smiles.

"So," Jamie said, looking at Carly with a grin. "You're coming to the wedding, right?"

THAT NIGHT, after they'd showered and made love, Reaper joined her beside the pond he'd dug in the front yard. The only forest-free space in the yard.

Carly bent to the silver trashcan beside the pond and scooped out the fish meal, replenishing the automatic pagoda-style feeder above the pond. Then holding pellets in her hand, she knelt beside the water to hold out her hand to the fish.

Just as the breeder promised them, the mature fish, familiar with hand-feeding set the example for the younger fish, who nibbled just as eagerly.

"You know we're gonna have bears swimming in there," he murmured. "They'll eat your fish."

"You don't think the alarm system will scare them off?" she said, eyeing the motion detector he'd flipped off before approaching the pond. When anything crossed the invisible boundary, a loud siren blared.

"I think they'll get used to it."

After glancing around, she frowned. "Then we'll have to build a fence. Put some dogs in the yard."

He gave an exaggerated sigh. "Those going on my Honey-Do List? Hell, building a fence will be easier than constructing that pool." He grumbled but didn't really begrudge the effort. They'd shared in the labor, digging the pit, lining it, and filling it with plants. The fact they'd found so many sources for the fish and pond supplies in the area had been eye-opening.

Carly stood and brushed her hands together. When she turned, her expression was hard to read.

Reaper held still as she drew closer.

She wrapped her arms around his waist and nestled against his chest. "You do know I was joking about you building a koi pond..."

He grunted and hugged her, relishing the feel of her body next to his. "I know."

She leaned back her head. "Then why do it?"

One side of his mouth curved up. "Because I knew every time you looked at your pond, you'd smile."

"You do know you don't fool me one bit." She poked a finger at his chest, just over his heart. "You, Reaper Stenberg, are a sweet, sweet man."

He narrowed his eyes. "Don't ever tell a soul."

"Think I would?" she said, her voice going husky. "You're my secret I won't ever share. There's plenty of you to go around, but I'm selfish. I'll keep you all to myself."

Reaper bent to kiss her. "Then make it forever, baby. Marry me?"

Fighting a smile, she rose up on her tiptoes and wrapped her arms around his neck. "Thought you weren't sure about this monogamy thing."

He rolled his eyes. "Will you ever just give me a straight answer?"

"Why should I?" she said, arching a brow. "I love what frustration makes you do."

"That taunting can work both ways, baby."

A slow smile stretched across her pretty face. "I won't break as easy as you do."

"We'll see." With that, he bent and bumped her belly with his shoulder.

Laughing, she folded over his back.

On the way up the steps, he felt her hands cup both sides of his ass.

As he climbed the porch and entered the house, Reaper mused. Loving Carly Wyatt had taught him a couple of things. One woman existed who could brighten every corner of his life. One woman made him believe in Happy-Ever-After. Who'd have thought it? Certainly not him, but he wasn't questioning fate or God or whatever force had placed Carly in his path. He'd just be grateful for the rest of his life.

Don't miss the next Montana Bounty Hunters book:
<u>Dagger</u>!

ABOUT DELILAH DEVLIN

Delilah Devlin is a *New York Times* and *USA TODAY* bestselling author with a rapidly expanding reputation for writing deliciously edgy stories with complex characters. She has published over one-hundred-eighty stories in multiple genres and lengths, and she has been published by Atria/Strebor, Avon, Berkley, Black Lace, Cleis Press, Ellora's Cave, Grand Central, Harlequin Spice, HarperCollins: Mischief, Kensington, Kindle, Kindle Worlds, Montlake Romance, Running Press, and Samhain Publishing.

You can find Delilah all over the web:
WEBSITE
BLOG
TWITTER
FACEBOOK FAN PAGE
PINTEREST

ABOUT DELILAH DEVLIN

Subscribe to her *newsletter* ***so you don't miss a thing!***
Or email her at: delilah@delilahdevlin.com

THE BOUNTY

A SHORT STORY IN THE MONTANA
BOUNTY HUNTERS WORLD

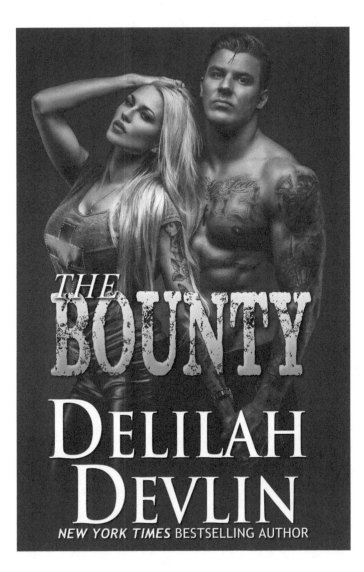

Enjoy reading the story that was my test run in the bounty-hunting world. Be warned, it's a tad "bluer" than Reaper! ~DD

The hunters I work with all have cool, dangerous-sounding handles: Catch, Dagger, Bulldog. My first day on the job, Bulldog nicknamed me Buttercup, and it stuck.

Catch, the hunter who founded this agency, decided he needed a bounty hunter with "soft" skills. Someone approachable, whom mamas and girlfriends could confide in. Not that he ever expected I'd have to do the "heavier" tasks, like break down a door or take a target to the ground. Bounty hunting's dangerous work, and not meant for faint-hearted dudes—or girls.

I felt lucky when they called me Buttercup because mostly they called me "the girl." Like this morning, when Catch handed out assignments and told Bulldog to take along *the girl*.

I didn't make a fuss. PC communications weren't part of any office handbook. I knew from day one I had to prove myself. Not that I'd gotten a chance, so far, to show them what I had. Being ex-military, and an ex-cop, didn't earn me any points. I guess it didn't help I was only five-feet-five and a hundred ten pounds soaking wet. Bulldog figured that with blonde hair and blue eyes, I looked more like a former high school cheerleader—not a compliment, since he thought girls like that were stupid as hell.

Maybe I didn't help my cause with the way I dressed. Ever since they'd named me Buttercup, I did my best to dress the part. Sure, I wore denim, tees, and boots, just like them, but my pink T-shirt emblazoned with "Girl Power," and my purple-calico-lined jean jacket with lace inserts on the pockets, didn't exactly fit with their black tees sporting bike club slogans and black leather jackets. The few times I hadn't been tied to a desk making phone calls to relatives to track low-lifes who'd skipped their court dates, I'd been relegated to staying in the truck while the guys did the dirty work.

Not so today, but only because we were going to reach out to Lenny Holcomb's mama to see if she wanted to keep her house, seeing as she'd offered her home as collateral when posting his bond.

Bulldog gave me the evil eye as we walked toward the small clapboard house on the bad side of town. "Shit goes sideways," he said, "you stand back and let me handle it."

I offered him a non-committal nod. "Think Mrs. Holcomb will give you that much trouble?"

He snorted and skewered me a narrow-eyed glare.

"Ooh," I said in my best little-girl voice and gave an exaggerated shiver, hoping he'd trip over his big feet. Not that I had to pretend my reaction too much. Something about the big burly guy did it for me. His face was too manly to be handsome—square jaw, crooked nose, laser-sharp blue eyes. Thick, gold-brown hair dusted the collar of his jacket. His six-foot-four, heavily-muscled frame made me feel feminine and soft and all those other useless qualities I despised in "helpless" females. Go figure—the thought of those big, hard hands rasping over my skin made me tremble.

At Mrs. Holcomb's door, I knocked.

No response.

I knocked again. Still nothing.

Bulldog stepped to the left and peered into the window. "Don't think anyone's home. And since this is his address of record…" He backed up and began to raise a booted foot.

I cleared my throat.

He lowered his foot and gave me a scowl.

"Really want to knock down her door?" I pulled my lock-pick kit from my back pocket and knelt in front of the knob. A couple of twists of my tools, and the lock snicked. I turned the knob and quickly moved away from the door, giving way to Bulldog as he grumbled something under his breath about smartass women and strode inside.

Bulldog's big frame filled my view, so I was taken by surprise when he cussed and rushed toward a hallway.

A crash sounded in a distant room. Light from an open doorway in the back glared as he ran through it. I followed, watching as our target ran for the chain link fence and vaulted over it.

Bulldog cussed again, placed a hand on the top of the fence, but when he swung over his big body, the thin metal rod running through the top caved, and he fell to the dirt.

I picked another spot farther down the fence, grabbed a post and swung over, landing on my booted feet and shooting down the alleyway.

Behind me, I heard grunts and more curses, and finally, "Dammit, Buttercup, wait for me!"

I wasn't waiting for shit. Lenny moved fast for a big boy. He was almost at the end of the alley. If I didn't catch him quickly, I'd lose sight of him, and we'd lose our paycheck. With my breaths coming fast and sweat trickling into my eyes, I sped up, reaching out with my fingertips to snatch a handful of his shirt. With the fabric in my fist, I drew back and swung him.

He went sideways, but he didn't go down. He twisted out of my grasp and raised his fists, his eyes widening as he looked me up and down, an ugly sneer stretching across his equally ugly face.

He swung.

But I was ready, ducking beneath and coming up to drive my fists into his fat gut, then bouncing backward to avoid the next wide swing.

When he didn't connect, his swing carried him forward, and he turned.

I rocketed to his back and wrapped my arm around his throat, grasping my fist to keep my arm in place, as he staggered then went to his knees, his fingers scratching my arms before reaching backward to pull my hair.

But he didn't get a hank. His body crashed forward, bringing me with him, because my arm was trapped beneath his thick neck. Then his body shifted halfway onto mine.

Boots pounded the pavement then slowed.

"Buttercup, need a hand?"

Not able to look back, I wheezed, trying to drag in a breath as Lenny's weight crushed me against the pavement. "Roll him so I can get back my arm."

Lenny's body rolled to his side.

Bulldog lowered his boot then bent to offer me a hand up. His gaze went to the thick scratches on my arms.

Blood ran in rivulets from the deep gouges.

"Goddammit." Bulldog's scowl was scary as he blew out a deep breath, and then reached behind his neck to pull his T-shirt over his head.

He tossed it at me.

All I could do was stare at the grayscale tattoos covering his shoulders and chest and disappearing into his jeans.

"Wrap this around your arm. You're gonna bleed all over my truck." Then he went down on one knee and locked cuffs around Lenny's fat wrists. When he stood, he kicked the low-life in the ass.

After we'd dropped Lenny at the jail, Bulldog remained silent as we drove.

My arm stung like hell, so I was fine with the quiet for the first while.

His expression was so dark, I didn't dare try to make small talk. When he missed the turnoff to the agency, I straightened and darted a glance his way. His narrowed gaze swung toward me, daring me to say a word. I sat back, my heart thudding hard inside my chest. Just how pissed was he?

Twenty minutes later, we pulled onto a gravel road. Once we passed the first curve, I saw a single-story house ahead. Gray stone and wood. A metal roof. He reached up to hit a button above his windshield, and a garage door rose.

So, this was his house. He'd brought me home. But would he cut me into tiny pieces and feed me to the Rottweiler jumping against the fence, or was he planning to read me the riot act in private, because he intended to yell and didn't want the world to hear?

I hoped for a third option. One where he pushed me face-down over the first piece of furniture we met and delivered his frustration in the sexiest way possible.

He pulled the SUV into the garage, hit the button to lower the door, and then turned to give me another glare. "Get the fuck inside."

I was tempted to chide him about his tone. Not his words. I wanted to be the fuck inside...*fucking*.

Without a word, I slipped out of the truck and headed to the wooden stairs leading into the house. I stepped inside a mud room then through another door and into the kitchen.

Bulldog entered behind me and closed the door.

His hands grasped my shoulders and turned me toward the table.

My heart stuttered—was this the bending over part? No, he pushed downward, forcing me into a chair.

"Unwrap your arm."

Disappointment turned the corners of my mouth downward. Slowly, because the shirt stuck to the bloody stripes, I peeled away the shirt while he headed toward the sink.

He ran water then pulled a washcloth from a drawer and wet it. Next, he strode back to the table, pulling out a chair to sit beside me. He laid the washcloth over my arm.

It was hot, and I winced.

"Got to soak the blood to loosen it," he said.

His voice was softer but no less growly, and my pulse raced.

When he wiped away the smears of blood, he shook his head. "Should have let him go, Buttercup. These'll leave scars."

I raised my chin. "Would you have?"

He grunted and completed his task, then stood, opened a cabinet above the stove, and pulled down a first aid kit. After he'd rubbed antiseptic gel over my wounds, he wrapped clean gauze around my arm and secured it with surgical tape.

"Thanks." I kept my eyes cast downward. "But I could have managed on my own."

"I know."

I lifted my head and found him studying me.

His mouth tightened. "You handled yourself well. I just didn't like you anywhere near that shithead."

"Oh." And because I was feeling off-kilter, his change in demeanor sending my insides swirling, I did what I always do when I feel a little afraid. I brazened it out, giving him a slow, seductive smile and a wink.

Instead of putting him back in his bad mood, his reaction to my taunt was a narrowing of his green eyes. He glanced at my mouth then shot out a hand and wrapped his fingers around the back of my neck to pull me toward him.

When his mouth slammed over mine, I gasped, giving him entry.

Bulldog might have been a big guy, but there was nothing lumbering or bearlike about his reactions. They were lightning fast. His tongue invaded my mouth, pushing past my teeth to stroke my tongue.

I gave a kitten-like mew, very un-me, and melted against him, my hand landing on his broad, bare chest, and my fingers tangling in his hair. Then he gripped my waist and slid me right off my chair onto his lap. Shock blasted through me at how much I liked the quick way he took charge.

He bent me backward, an arm around my shoulders. His free hand slipped between my legs and pushed against the damp denim, cupping me then squeezing my sex. "You're fucking wet, Buttercup," he rasped when he raised his head to let me breathe. Then slowly, daring me with his steady stare, he removed his hand from my crotch and cupped my breast through my clothing. "This okay with you?"

I managed a nod, and before I drew another breath, he went to his feet, with me in his arms, and strode through the house, past a living room filled with deep leather seating, down a hallway, and into a bedroom. His bed was enormous, an Alaska or a Wyoming-size King. He crawled onto the mattress on his knees and stepped toward the center before he set me down. Then he began stripping away my holster, my belt...my tee and bra...my shoes and pants. When the only thing I wore was a pair of bikini panties, he halted, backed off the bed, and began stripping off his own clothing, flinging each piece to the side while he kept his hungry stare on me.

But I wasn't any woman waiting on a man to decide what happened next. I lifted my bottom, scraped down my panties, and threw them at his face.

Magnificently nude, he leapt toward the bed, diving toward the middle.

I rolled away, and just had my feet on the floor, when his arms wrapped around my waist, and he pulled me back against his body. He sat on the edge of the mattress and bracketed my legs with his thick thighs, then smoothed his rough palms over my skin, starting at my breasts then moving down my belly to my pussy. I squirmed in his arms trying to turn, but he kept me faced away as he felt me up, sending tingles through me.

Again, he cupped my breasts, and I felt his tongue slide from the center of my back upward, following my spine. Goose bumps prickled on my skin. My breaths grew short. *Fuck, oh fuck.* I wanted him. "Bulldog," I said, shivering hard inside his embrace.

"Don't fight me, Buttercup. Don't move. Let me do you the way I have to."

He turned me until I faced him.

I stood with my arms at my sides as he raked my body with his gaze. His for the taking, because I wanted to be taken.

I couldn't resist dropping my gaze to his cock, so thick and straight, jerking against his belly to the beat of his heart.

"Fuck, oh fuck," I whispered and shivered hard again.

He reached to the side, slid open a drawer in the nightstand, and pulled out a condom. With his lips pulling back from his teeth, he cloaked himself, then scooted backward on the bed and patted the mattress beside him.

I crawled toward him then lay on my belly beside him, hiding my face against the coverlet, because I knew my expression would give away just how badly I wanted this. I rubbed on the mattress, because my skin burned and my nipples ached.

He kissed my shoulder and climbed over me, his weight pressing me deep into the mattress as he fisted his hand in my hair and held me down, then slipped his legs, one at a time between mine, waiting for me to open to him.

When he rooted his cock between my legs, my breath shuddered out. His lower body scooped against me, rubbing against my ass as he teased me with the tip of his cock sliding between my slick folds.

His teeth dragged on my earlobe, and he whispered, "I'm gonna fuck you up, babe. Fuck hard and deep. You ready, Buttercup?"

I made a sound—half-laugh, half-sob. *Ready?* Never. But I quivered underneath him and strained to lift my ass, needing him to take me now.

With one hand still lodged in my hair, he lifted his hips and slid his free arm beneath my waist to raise my hips.

I braced on my knees, my belly barely off the bed, because that's all the room he gave me, and then he was rutting against me, pushing between my folds, quick in and out slides, penetrating only a couple of inches.

"Don't tease," I said, hissing when he tightened his fingers on my hair. My scalp stung, but the pain only made the tension winding inside my core tighten more. Already, my lips were clenching, releasing, trying to capture his cockhead as he wet it in the fluid drenching my sex.

"You want this," he whispered, pushing a little deeper then withdrawing.

Way past worrying about my pride, I whimpered. "Yes. Yes, please."

"One thing, babe. One thing before I give it to you. Promise me."

My pulse pounded in my ears. "Anything, just please, Bulldog…"

He nuzzled into the hair beside my ear. "Don't ever scare me like that again."

He pushed inside then rotated his hips, his fat head dragging around my entrance. "Promise."

"Anything."

"Mean it."

I could have lied and told him what he wanted to hear. And I was tempted, but lying wasn't in me. "I...can't." I wanted to cry. Wanted to shout. But his weight crushed me, making breathing hard.

He let go of my hair and moved away.

I pushed to my elbows, but I couldn't look behind me. I'd never been torn down like that, reduced to quivering and begging. Not by any man. "I should leave," I whispered.

The bed shifted beside me. He lay on his back beside me, an arm beneath his head, his gaze on the ceiling above.

I glanced down his body and noted with not a little disappointment that his cock was still rigid, so heavy it rested on his firm belly. "You had no right to ask me that," I said, staring at his dick and knowing my expression was shattered.

He tucked his thumb under my chin and turned my head to meet his gaze. "You'll make an old man of me."

"Then ask Catch to reassign me to ride with someone else," I said, my voice surly.

Frowning, he shook his head. "Doesn't solve a damn thing."

"You think I'm a problem to solve?" I pushed up to sit on my folded legs, not caring his glance roamed my nude body. "You're the one with the problem. I have a job I *know* I can do well. Do you have any idea what I've faced? Being a woman in the Army, now a hunter with a bunch of misogynists? You may call me Buttercup, but

I'm not some delicate princess. I know you spent time in the sandbox. And you know damn well, I did, too. And I wasn't serving any damn coffee to some general in the Green Zone."

Bulldog's face tightened. "I know you're capable. That you can handle yourself, but shit..." His gaze went to the bandage on my arm. He shook his head and rubbed a hand over his face. "For that minute when I was picking myself up off the ground, and I lost sight of you..."

Again, he shook his head and speared me with a look so stark my ready retort dried on my lips.

"So, you were worried about me. Maybe tomorrow, I'll be worried about you. Sounds like we'll both lose some sleep."

He blinked. The corners of his mouth twitched. "We losing that sleep together?" he drawled.

"Depends on you, shithead." I cupped my breasts and jiggled them. "You're the one who climbed off this."

"Come here."

I narrowed my gaze. "I'm not making any damn promises."

"And I'll learn to deal. But you'll have to get used to this—me working out my...*issues*, when you do something that hits me square in the gut."

I held still for a second, and then gave him a slow smile. "Maybe you shouldn't give me incentives to make sure you get *issues* to work out on my ass."

One wicked brow arched. "Does your ass feel neglected?"

Done with waiting for him to get over himself, I

leaned back, braced on my hands, and stretched out my legs, spreading them to offer an unencumbered view of what his dick was still hard for. "Better get up inside me, Bulldog, or I'll see if Dagger needs a new partner."

With his abs flexing, he sat, then climbed over me, not stopping his upward crawl until his cock nudged my pussy. "You'll ride with me," he said, his voice hard. "Where I can keep an eye out."

"Show me why I should choose you," I whispered.

His chest jerked on a grunt. "Do you ever stop?"

I puckered my lips and blew him a kiss. "No. Can you deal with this mouth?"

His lips landed on mine, effectively proving he could, and very well, as he devoured my mouth.

With the way he chose to fight, the horny part of me hoped I'd never win an argument.

I raised my knees to bracket his hips then scraped my fingernails from his shoulders to his hard ass. Without raising his body to make room between us, he entered me with a slow roll of his hips.

My mouth went slack beneath his as I reveled in the way he filled me, his girth stretching my inner walls. When he was all the way inside, he lifted his head and nipped my nose and my chin. "Buttercup, for a girl with such a big mouth, your pussy's just a little thing."

I pinched his ass. "Not delicate. Move!"

He chuckled, his upper body jerking against mine.

Right then, I might have smiled, but he slipped his hands under my ass and began rocking against me, sliding in and out, while his body ground against mine, heating the skin of my breasts and belly.

I needed him to give me space to let me move, needed him to get on his knees so he could stroke me with deeper, longer thrusts. More than that, I needed my clit rubbed, or I'd never come. Frustrated, I glared upward.

His smile was sly. He knew he was driving me crazy.

I lifted my lips in a snarl. "You want something..."

"I do."

"You've already got me naked. You're already inside me."

"Baby, I just decided I want more."

I widened my glare and slipped a finger into the crease of his ass.

Again, showing surprising speed, he slipped his hands from beneath me, grabbed my arms, and moved them upward. "I want you to agree that when we're here, in this bed, you'll do whatever I want."

I shrugged. "Will whatever you want give me what I want?"

"Eventually."

I pursed my lips and frowned. "And what do you want right now?"

His gaze dropped to my mouth.

"Huh. I'm down with that," I said, my voice dropping to a husky whisper. Sure, it wouldn't have taken much to push me into an orgasm, a flick of a nail against my clit, but I was curious about he'd feel inside my mouth...for starters.

"I'm gonna pull out now, but I want you to stay still. Agreed?"

At my nod, he slid slowly from within me, then knelt beside me and rolled off his condom. "I'm clean, Buttercup," he said, fisting his shaft and giving it a long pull.

I liked seeing his big hand slide on his rigid cock. "Me, too. And on the pill. Just so you know." I swallowed then licked my lips because my mouth was drying up—likely because it had hung open so long as I'd stared at him fisting himself. Something about watching him pump his generous man-meat, the sight glorified by the background of his muscled body, covered in gray-and-black tattoos of skulls festooned with flowers and guns, made me feel very, very feminine.

Here in his bed, just as I'd agreed, I'd do anything he wanted so long as I could touch every inch of his skin...suck every inch of his hard cock...

He lay on his back and held his cock so it pointed at the ceiling. "Your mouth on me..."

I scrambled up to kneel by his side.

But he shook his head and held out his arms. "Your pussy on my mouth..."

Better and better. I angled my body around and slowly lifted a knee over his head. With his hands guiding me, I spread myself and lowered, then gasped as his mouth latched on my labia, sucking and nibbling on my folds.

He slid a hand over my ass and smacked it, reminding me of my task.

Braced on one hand, I used the other to grip him at

the base and lowered my mouth to suck his head. I swirled my tongue around and around, learning the territory and sliding into his tiny slit.

His musky scent and taste made me hungrier, and I opened wide and glided downward, loving the feel of him sliding on my tongue as I went deep. When the cap touched the back of my throat, I swallowed, the action giving him a sexy caress that made him groan against my sex.

His fingers entered me. His tongue slid to my clit, slicking over it. Then fingers lifted the top of my folds, pulling away the hood protecting my swelling knot of nerves.

I opened my throat and sank deeper, giving him everything he could want, just so he'd keep doing what he was—tapping, rubbing, flicking—until my thighs and belly quivered.

Mouth stuffed, I breathed noisily through my nostrils, little whimpers escaping as he fingered me. When he sucked my clit, I gave a very muffled shout. He had me on the edge, but I wanted his permission, his encouragement, before I flew. I wanted to please him more than I wanted my own pleasure.

Bulldog released my clit and kissed it. Then he withdrew his fingers. "I want you on your hands and knees," he said, his voice rough and tight.

I came off him, trailed my tongue one last time up his shaft, then quickly crawled sideways, still faced away and waiting.

His hands gripped my ass and spread my cheeks. "Everything's red and wet," he rasped.

I sank my belly to lift my ass and braced my arms.

When he nudged my pussy, I bit my lower lip to still a cry. When he pushed inside, I arched deeper, clutching my own hair, waiting as he screwed slowly inside, swirling around and around, until his groin was snug against me.

I reached beneath me and gripped his balls, fondling the warm, heavy sac.

His thumbs slid into my crack and pressed on my tiny, puckered hole. "That ass is mine, Buttercup."

A promise I'd make him keep. "Yes."

Then he gripped the notches of my hips and strained inward. "This pussy is mine."

"Yes." I glanced sideways at the mirror above his dresser. I liked what I saw—every muscle of his body defined as he held himself there behind me. So big and ridiculously masculine.

Then there was no time to admire the picture we made—hard and soft, large and small—because he began to move, pushing me away as he withdrew, bringing me back with a snap as he thrust forward. Nothing gentle about his fucking. Hard, harsh—each muscular thrust rattling my teeth.

Slow, at first. Then faster. His cock tunneled, heating my core. Tension coiled deep inside me, making it hard to catch my breath. I grunted and moaned. Until I sobbed.

His balls banged against the top of my folds, each

bounce a tease. But I didn't dare fiddle with my clit. That was his right. And I knew he'd take it when he was ready. Already, he'd proven he knew what I liked. What I needed.

My breasts quivered with his strokes, the tips hard as pebbles and aching. My pussy spasmed around him, my channel convulsed...wet...so wet, the sounds of his flesh hitting mine grew louder and sloppier.

When at last he shortened his thrusts and bent to reach around me, I tossed back my hair and stiffened, ready. *Now, now, now...*

He bent farther while he kept stroking and nuzzled the corner of my neck. "Now, baby. *Fuck, now.*"

He gave my engorged clit a twist.

I shattered, keening as he emptied himself inside me. The cry I emitted long and thin.

Long moments later, I was still dragging air into my lungs and shivering.

Bulldog wrapped his arms around me, then bracing an arm on the bed, brought us both down, his cock still lodged inside me.

We lay on our sides, his hands caressing my breasts. The weight of his arm against my waist felt...right. Somehow comforting.

A kiss landed on my shoulder. "Fucking unbelievable," he whispered.

I grinned. Though my injured arm was beginning to throb and I was tired, I didn't want to sleep. I wanted to bask in the moment and catalog every sensation—the hot palms squeezing my tits, the waning thickness locking our bodies together, his large, bearish frame snuggled against my back. "Think you might want to do that again?" I asked, surprised that my voice sounded so girly, so needy. My heart tripped as I wondered whether I'd pressed for too much.

Bulldog bit my shoulder then eased away.

Without being told, I turned and rested my head on his arm. He pressed me closer until my breasts rested against his chest. Then he slid a hairy thigh between mine. Again, I was surrounded by his body.

His gaze was on the fingers that played with a nipple, where a thumb rubbed lazily across it. "We ride together. We sleep together."

I appreciated his simplistic speech. To the point. Reassuring. "I liked today," I said. "Everything about it."

"Even our argument?"

One side of my mouth twitched upward. "I like the way you ended it. But..." I waited until his gaze rose to lock with mine. "This doesn't mean I'll be so easy at work."

"Think you're easy?" He laughed. "My dick's a fucking nub."

I reached down and gripped his "nub." "And now, I have high expectations," I drawled as I gave it a gentle tug.

He grimaced. "I'd just as soon not let the other guys know."

I narrowed my eyes. "Because you're embarrassed?"

"No, because they'll be all over me, asking me how good you are in bed."

I gave his nub another, not-so-gentle tug. "What would you tell them?"

"I don't fuck and tell, babe, but if I did…" He flicked my nipple with a nail. "I'd tell them you're the best I've ever had."

I let go of his cock and snuggled closer to his chest. "Is that the truth?"

"I won't ever lie."

I guessed by his lowering eyebrows that he was waiting for me to respond in kind. "Don't go getting a big head," I said, sliding my gaze away, because truth-time made me uncomfortable. I rubbed my palm over his heart and thought about what I wanted to say. Something to tell him just how pleased I was with him as a lover, but something that would also tell him that this, for me, hadn't just been about fucking. Somewhere along the way, I'd started feeling something… more. "I'd like to try this, Bulldog."

"Chris."

I blinked.

"Just because I want you to say my name doesn't mean I'll stop calling you Buttercup."

I pressed my lips together to keep from grinning. He'd saved me from getting all mushy, but at the same time, he'd told me—with just one word, his name—that he wanted to be closer, too. "Chris." Taking a deep breath, I finally met his gaze.

He was smiling.

Maybe it was a bit smirky, but he'd earned the right to feel proud of himself.

I inched my thigh upward until I nudged his balls. Then I arched a brow in challenge.

Bulldog growled deep in his chest and rolled over me, trapping me with his weight. "Sure you can take more?"

"Again," I said breathlessly. "Not delicate."

A week later, we pulled into a far corner of a parking lot outside a biker bar that Sparky Leonard's ex-girlfriend had named as his favorite haunt.

"His bike's here, all right," Bulldog muttered as he stared down the long line of bikes parked in front of the bar.

"And you know that, how?"

He shrugged. "I ride with his club sometimes."

I frowned, trying to see inside the window, but we were too far away and the glass proved too dirty. "They know where you work?"

"I might have mentioned it."

I shook my head. "Then you can't go in first. Everyone will know straight away why you're there."

Sparky had failed to show up for his regularly scheduled drug test. Our job was to deliver him straight to jail.

"Not how this works, Buttercup."

"So you keep saying." I didn't glance his way as I took off my jacket then wrestled under my shirt to remove my bra. I pulled the band from my ponytail and shook my hair around my shoulders. Then I opened my jeans and tucked in the tee, tightly enough the tips of my boobs were clearly visible.

"What are you doing?"

I removed my holster and stuffed my weapon in the glove box. Then I shoved handcuffs in the back pocket of my jeans. "Give me a couple of minutes before you come inside. I'll get close to him."

He reached out and wrapped his fingers around my upper arm.

I stared down at his hand then lifted my head to give him a steely glare.

Only he didn't begin reading me the riot act, telling me how this would go down—me waiting in the truck while he took down the bad guy. Instead, he pulled my upper body over the console between us and kissed me silly.

When he released me, he gave me a wink. "Two minutes. Tops."

I touched my puffy lips as I headed inside, sure everyone there could tell how turned on I was. Sure enough, my chest got whistles.

Sparky was sitting at the bar, his thinning red hair peeking out from beneath the blue bandana he wore Axl-Rose style around his head. As I approached, his gaze locked on my chest.

I paused beside him and leaned over the arm he held extended toward his beer, making sure my breast brushed his skin as I pretended to seek the bartender's attention.

"Hey, sweet thing," he said, his gaze going from my boobs to my eyes.

"Hey, yourself." I gave him a slow wink.

He cleared his throat and sat straighter. "Can I get you a drink?"

I leaned closer, trying not to wrinkle my nose at the smell of stale sweat. "No, but you can place your arms behind you."

"I can?" he asked, his gaze falling again to my tits as I rubbed them on his chest then on his arm as I circled behind him. Then I reached into my back pocket, pulled out the cuffs, deftly slapped them open, and clicked one around his wrist.

"Baby, you don't have to do that," he whined. "I woulda said yes."

Around him, laughter started as his buddies figured out quicker than he did that he wasn't about to get lucky. Maybe they knew because Bulldog was making a beeline toward me, his gaze smoldering.

Had he seen me cozy up to Sparky?

I grabbed Sparky's other wrist and pulled it back. The second cuff secure, I pushed him off the stool. "Time to go, baby."

Bulldog growled and gripped Sparky's upper arm, yanking him away.

As I followed the two men, I swung my hips, grinning as whistles followed me out the door.

After Bulldog helped Sparky into the back seat of the SUV, he slammed the door then rounded on me. His hands shot out and gripped my hips to pull me against his body.

The kiss that landed on my mouth ground my lips

against my teeth, but I didn't mind. I slid a hand over the front of his jeans.

He jerked back and handed me the keys. "Drive."

He never let me drive, but I got it. He didn't want my unfettered boobs anywhere near Sparky's person. I sauntered to the driver's door and let myself in. Then I adjusted the seat and mirror, dipping it low enough I could lock gazes with my man.

"Bulldog, she's yours?" Sparky asked, his voice a tinny whine.

"All mine."

"Damn. Are her tits for real?"

"Sparky—" Bulldog gritted out. "You want to keep your teeth, you won't mention my girl's tits again."

The rest of the drive was made in silence. Bulldog insisted I remain in the car while he took care of Sparky and the paperwork inside the jail. I figured he didn't want anyone else seeing my assets bounce.

When he returned, he eyed me through the windshield, and I quickly climbed over the console into the passenger seat. Before my butt hit the leather, he slammed the door.

Five minutes later, he pulled into a small gas station and escorted me straight into the restroom in the back. Inside five seconds, he had my jeans around my knees. Then he bent me over in front of the sink and fucked me.

After we both came hard, we bought sodas and took a more leisurely route to the agency with our hands clasped atop the console.

"That was fun." I rolled my head on the headrest to

glance at his profile. Bumpy nose, heavy brows, square chin. All manly muscle. I sighed.

"Next time," he said, lowering his voice into that gravely growl I was coming to love, "don't give me a hard-on before we make the grab."

I huffed a breath. I wasn't making a promise I couldn't keep.

ALSO BY DELILAH DEVLIN

Montana Bounty Hunters Series

Reaper (#1)

Dagger (#2)

Texas Billionaires Club

Tarzan & Janine (#1)

Something to Talk About (#2)

Who's Your Daddy (#3)

Love & War (#4)

Short Story Collections

Warrior's Conquest

Rogues

Enslaved by the Viking Short Story

Conquests

Smokin' Hot Firemen

Made in United States
Troutdale, OR
01/04/2024

16696990R00100